RANGER WADE

To Marjorie
God Bless

Jeanne Murnette Smith

RANGER WADE

Jeannie Murnette Smith

TATE PUBLISHING
AND ENTERPRISES, LLC

Ranger Wade
Copyright © 2015 by Jeannie Murnette Smith. All rights reserved.

No part of this publication may be reproduced, stored in a retrieval system or transmitted in any way by any means, electronic, mechanical, photocopy, recording or otherwise without the prior permission of the author except as provided by USA copyright law.

This novel is a work of fiction. Names, descriptions, entities, and incidents included in the story are products of the author's imagination. Any resemblance to actual persons, events, and entities is entirely coincidental.

The opinions expressed by the author are not necessarily those of Tate Publishing, LLC.

Published by Tate Publishing & Enterprises, LLC
127 E. Trade Center Terrace | Mustang, Oklahoma 73064 USA
1.888.361.9473 | www.tatepublishing.com

Tate Publishing is committed to excellence in the publishing industry. The company reflects the philosophy established by the founders, based on Psalm 68:11,
"The Lord gave the word and great was the company of those who published it."

Book design copyright © 2015 by Tate Publishing, LLC. All rights reserved.
Cover design by Niño Carlo Suico
Interior design by Mary Jean Archival

Published in the United States of America

ISBN: 978-1-68207-228-8
Fiction / Action & Adventure
15.10.02

Dedicated to the USA warriors that have, are, and will put their lives in danger to protect the freedom that makes the United Stated of America the great nation that it is. I pray for them every day. I give thanks to the guys and girls who served, are serving, and will serve.

1

Reaching desperately for air, the huge Alsatian staggered the last few yards to the cabin just south of the ranger station and collapsed on the steps.

Panting heavily for a few seconds, he struggled to his feet, staggered to the door, and scratched with both paws, barking frantically. The door swung open, and the man standing there was a welcome sight to the frantic animal. Barking urgently, the dog turned to go and turned back to the man again.

"Well hi, Shade, you seem to be upset about something."

Barking again urgently, Shade turned to go then turned back to the man once more.

"You want me to follow you…? Okay, hang on a minute." Turning back into the cabin, the man quickly gathered a few things to handle a possible emergency, and grabbing his gun, he strapped it on. Stepping out of the cabin, he motioned to the jeep. "Might as well take the jeep. You look like you came a ways." Opening the door, he stepped aside and waited for Shade to jump in and climbed in after him.

Watching the dog, Ranger Sergeant Wade McKenna turned the jeep in the direction he was looking and gave it the gas. Still panting heavily in spite of the chilly day, Shade kept his eyes on the road that he had just come over; and when he whined and strained to the left, Wade braked, backed, and turned left. Settled and watching ahead once more, they continued this way for the next three miles until Shade lunged at the window and barked. Braking, Wade turned the motor off, set the brake, and opened the jeep's door.

Having lived with dogs most of his life, Wade could read their actions pretty good, and Shade's were something he could not ignore. The huge black-and-silver German shepherd weighed in a bit over 127 pounds and was gentle with children and women but didn't usually trust men until he knew them well. Wade was an old family friend and had played with him as a puppy. He was mostly silver with a darker shading on his muzzle and back, making him look a bit like a timber wolf.

Leaping to the ground soon as the door was opened, Shade made a beeline for the edge of the bluff overlooking the Flathead River and looked down then back at Wade, whining anxiously.

Shutting the jeep door, Wade followed and edging close to the drop-off. He hung on to a small hickory tree and leaned out to see closer onto the bluff's side. The unusual bit of color caught his eye, and he quickly identified it as a pair of jeans belonging to a small woman or child, he thought. The legs were all that he could see, and they weren't moving. The child or woman had fallen about fifty feet, probably hitting several rocks on the way, which might have slowed the fall a bit but didn't do him—or her—any good.

"Oh Lord, that has to be little Patty Beal," Wade groaned. "Patty! Can you hear me? Can you move? Patty!"

No movement; she was unconscious…or dead. He groaned again mentally. She was the only child of his best friend and partner Jess Beal. If he and his wife lost Patty, it would kill them.

Quickly returning to the jeep, he used the radio to notify the hospital in the nearest town of Columbia Falls of the situation. It would take a while for help to arrive as Columbia Falls was at least twenty miles away.

With the promise of help on the way, Wade grabbed the rope that was a permanent part of the jeep's equipment, and tying it off to the same hickory he had used to get his look-see, he quickly lowered himself to the motionless child. Reaching her side, careful not to move her, he pulled the brush away and noted that she was breathing slowly but steadily. Untying the blanket that he had brought with him, he spread it over the motionless child and waited for help to arrive.

Only seven years old, he was not surprised to find her alone with only a dog for company. For the most part, she grew up in wilderness areas, and they were her playground.

She loved nature and planned on being a forest ranger just like her dad and her friend Wade. She was born in the ranger cabin that Jess and Sue Beal lived in, with the help of Wilma Blessons, the secretary that took care of the paperwork at the ranger station. Lucky that Wilma had the training to help, or they would have been up a creek without a paddle as Patricia Sue Beal didn't wait for the help they had called for to arrive. She was twelve minutes old and screaming her head off when they arrived, getting a grin from the paramedic. "Sounds like he's doing a hundred."

"She," the new mother corrected. She grimaced. "I sounded like that a little while ago."

The paramedics had checked them both and transported them to the hospital for a complete checkup by a physician.

Twenty-two minutes later, Wade heard the distant sirens of the medical unit and a sheriff's deputy as they topped the bluff road. And within minutes, the ambulance slammed to a stop by Wade's jeep with the deputy pulling up close by. Yelling to direct them to the victim, Wade watched the paramedics head appear beside the tied off rope. Asking a few pertinent questions, he disappeared and then was back and climbing down the rope that Wade had left hanging. The paramedic quickly checked Patty's life signs. Stabilizing her leg and arm after he put on the neck brace, he checked her vitals again before signaling his partner to send down the stretcher. He strapped Patty in carefully and, with Wade and his partner's help, lifted the still-unconscious child to the top of the bluff.

At Wade's impatient question, the paramedic finished putting Patty on oxygen then told him what he could.

"She shows signs of a concussion, a broken leg and arm, and possible internal injuries. Won't know for sure till she's x-rayed and checked by a physician. She's lucky to be alive after a fall like that. The brush she fell into helped. The rocks she hit slowed her fall on the way down, but that's probably what broke her arm and leg and gave her the head injury. That's all I can tell you. You coming with her?"

"Can't," Wade admitted. "I have her bicycle, the jeep, and a dog to see to, and the deputy is going to want some answers as to what happened," he replied, nodding toward the patiently waiting officer. "I'll stop by the hospital soon as I let the Beals know about Patty."

Nodding, the paramedic climbed in the back to stay with Patty, and as Wade shut the rear doors of the ambulance, the driver started for the hospital as fast as the road permitted. Wade had found her bike several yards from the road propped against a tree. After talking to the deputy for several minutes and answering what questions he could, he watched him follow the ambulance out and, looking up at the green canopy above, sent up a silent prayer for Patty's recovery.

Loading Patty's bike into the back of the jeep, Wade called to Shade. Petting the still-anxious dog, Wade said, "I know you're worried, boy, but she's in good hands now. With the Good Lord's help, she'll be okay. Come on, I'll give you a ride home. I got to tell her folks about her accident anyway." He added grimly, "Not something I'm looking forward to."

At age thirty-two, six foot four, 210 pounds and one-fourth Cherokee, Ranger Sergeant Wade McKenna could handle most anything he came up against. But something like this left him feeling helpless, a feeling he didn't like one little bit. Being a mix between rugged and handsome, without an ounce of excess weight, with straight black hair that seemed to always be a bit long, and with a permanent tan from being outdoors most of the time plus possessing steel-gray eyes, he could choose among the ladies that showed interest in him—and most of them did—but he dated very seldom. His ranger duties took up most of his time, and he loved to fish, ski, and visit his family when he had time off. Thinking about people living in crowded cities and breathing car exhaust, walking on hot concrete, and living in the beehives they called buildings—when compared to the cool, peaceful green forest—simply suffocated him. He tried not to think about it. He never visited a city unless he absolutely had to; then he made the visit short as he could manage without showing bad manners.

Taking a deep breath, he let it out slowly and got in the jeep after Shade and left the accident area. He would rather take a beating than tell Jess and Sue about Patty, but it had to be done.

Shutting the jeep door after Shade jumped in, Wade circled to the other side and climbed in behind the wheel. Sitting for a few minutes, Wade tried to find a way to let Patty's parents know about her accident. Talking it over with Shade didn't help a bit, he thought disgustedly, too one-sided. Besides, he finally admitted to himself, he was just putting it off. He would simply have to bite the bullet and get it over with. An anxious whine from Shade brought him out of his procrastination, and with a quick rub between the dog's ears, he put the jeep in gear, and Wade drove off.

2

"I only turned my back for a minute!" the distraught secretary moaned into her damp handkerchief. "I sat her down with milk and cookies and turned to give information to campers, and when I turned back, she was gone. I checked all around the headquarters building, but there was no sign of her. Everyone was out on patrol, and I was alone, I couldn't abandon the place, I just didn't know what to do. I called to see if you and Jess were back yet, but no one answered. I called Ranger Wade's cabin, but he was gone also. All I could do was wait."

Sue put her arm around the secretary's heaving shoulders and murmured in an effort to comfort the woman. "Oh, Wilma, she moves fast when she wants to, you're not to blame. Please don't take on so, you'll make yourself sick. I should have warned you about that when we asked you to watch her, but we had so much on our minds that it simply didn't occur to us. After all day in school, she was ready for exercise. If Peggy had had her accident tomorrow instead of last night, we could have taken her with us, but she had already left for school this morning when we got the word. I appreciate you taking her in until we could get back. She would have been safe from anything but falling. We trust Shade completely. Besides, the doctor expects a complete recovery. She'll need nursing for a while, but the accident just might have a cautioning effect on her...I hope!"

"Not your fault, Wilma, please calm yourself." Jess agreed. "If we hadn't been in such a hurry, we would have given you more information on her habits. She is pretty wild, but that has come to an end...at least for a while." He grimaced.

Wiping her eyes with the soggy handkerchief, Wilma finally managed to stop crying and, after a few more sniffles, asked, "How is your sister, is she going to be all right?"

"She lucked out," Sue returned, still pale from the shock of almost losing two of her family. "A truck driver saw the accident and pulled her out of the car before the fire reached her. A drunk driver hit the driver's side a glancing blow, knocking her off the road, and kept going. The police caught him later. Her car rolled down the slope and wound up against a large oak tree. A sudden stop, but it kept her from winding up in the river. The truck driver who saw the accident got his partial plate instead of full plate and the make of his car as he stopped to help Peggy. The drunk guy has several DWI convictions on his record. This time he will spend time in jail.

Peg has a broken left shoulder, bruised ribs, and a crack in her left thigh bone, a beautiful shiner on her left eye, and various other bruises but will recover. Her car is a total loss." Sue gave a gulp and lost most of her remaining color at the thought of losing her twin sister. When her parents found they were to be parents, they planned on Peggy Sue for a girl. When twin girls came along, they each got one of the names.

Hugging her as he watched her pale face with concern, Jess murmured softly, "That turned out all right also. Maybe we could bring her here and take care of her and Patty together. They can complain to each other when we need some rest," Jess said, grinning hopefully.

"Oh, Jess, that's a wonderful idea!" Sue agreed enthusiastically, some of her color returning. "When do you think the doctors will release her so we can go get her?"

Looking surprised, Jess replied, "I'll find out," and watched his wife hurry into Patty's hospital room to let her know that her Aunt Peggy was coming for a long visit.

"I was kidding," Jess said mournfully. "Was just trying to cheer her up."

His short red hair stuck out in all directions from having his fingers run through it, which is something he always did when upset about something. Sue didn't tell him that was how she always knew when something bothered him. He thought it was womanly intuition or something.

Scrubbing his hand down the length of his face, Jess moaned, "My mama said there would be days like this, but she didn't say they came in bunches!"

Getting her sense of humor back, Wilma smirked. "Stuck your foot in it, didn't you?" The fifty-eight-year-old, five-foot-four, slightly overweight, sweet-tempered, blue-eyed blond widow with the cherubic face took a deep breath and let it out slowly, trying to bring her stress level down. Finding out that Patty would be all right helped. Her doctor would have a field day chewing her out about her blood pressure right about now, she thought. Probably insist on her taking the medicine they had been after her to take for the last two years. She'd refused as she hadn't liked the side effects. If she had to take medicine for her blood pressure, maybe the doctor could prescribe something else that didn't have the side effects. She admitted that she should have asked him about that before. *Oh well, "should haves" don't count*, she thought philosophically. "If things like this keep happening though, I might just have to have another shot at it." Picking up her purse and jacket, she said her good-byes and, stepping outside the hospital door, took a deep breath of the clean Montana air. Fortified, Wilma thanked the Good Lord that Patty was going to be all right and added thanks for Sue's sister also. Then climbing into her car, she headed back to the ranger station where Sergeant McKenna was holding down the fort.

Wade hated paperwork but had promised to watch things while Wilma visited Patty. He had wanted to visit her also, but someone had to stay with the ranger station; and with the captain at a conference, that was Wilma or himself. As Wilma felt responsible for Patty's accident and needed to see that she was all right, he had volunteered to stay.

Just having nearly lost her sister, when Wade gave Jess and Sue the news about Patty, Sue almost fainted. Jess turned pale but did his best to comfort his wife while finding out what he could about the accident and Patty's condition. Wade told him what the paramedic had said, and when they hurriedly left for the hospital, Wade had headed for the ranger station to give Wilma an update about Patty.

This is not a day that I would like to repeat! he thought grimly, remembering Wilma's reaction to the news of Patty's accident.

After Wilma had settled down a bit, Wade volunteered to take over so she could visit the hospital. Gratefully, she had hurriedly grabbed her jacket and purse and left. An hour and a half later, Wade admitted volunteering for anything was idiotic. You'd think by now he'd know better.

Two groups of campers and four hikers crowded the station, and all wanted information, brochures, maps, and a list of camping and hiking rules. Wade couldn't find anything and was getting quite desperate when Wilma walked in the door… he felt like kissing her. "My turn to visit Patty," he said and, grabbing his hat, left posthaste.

"Well hi, good-bye, and thanks!" she said to the closing door, getting grins from several of the campers.

Saying a prayer of thanks that everyone was going to be all right, Wilma took control of the crowd and soon had everyone satisfied and on their way.

It being Friday, the campers and hikers were coming in droves. Glacier National Park was a camper's dream with its animal and bird life, crystal-clear air, and breathtaking scenery. Sighing deeply, she went into the kitchen in the back and made herself a cup of coffee. Taking a swallow, she sighed, "Ahh, I needed that." She grinned; caffeine was something else that her doctor frowned on her using.

She usually limited herself to one cup in the morning, but today was anything but usual; and holding up her cup, she toasted the doctor who was trying so hard to keep her healthy. Carrying her cup back to the front office, she dug into her neglected workload. She only worked here two days a week, but it helped pay the bills. Besides, she liked the people at the ranger station, and it got a bit lonely at home sometimes since she lost her husband to colon cancer two years ago. She baked regularly and brought most of her baking to the ranger station, or she would weigh a lot more than she did, she figured. *Spoiling them rotten too*, she thought fondly.

Hurrying to his jeep, Wade took a deep breath of the pine-laden air. "Just wasn't meant to be an inside ranger," he muttered. Climbing in, he shut the door and started the jeep. Pulling away from the ranger station, he headed for the hospital to visit his favorite little buddy.

3

Stepping out of the shower the next morning, Wade grabbed a towel and scrubbed his dripping hair vigorously then tackled the rest of his muscular body.

Remembering his last shower, Wade grimaced—it was when Wilma said she called him when Patty went missing. He had to have been taking his shower about then. Was no wonder he hadn't heard the phone ring. Shade had come for help about an hour and fifteen minutes after Patty had taken off. Shaking his head, he threw the wet towel over the shower door and grabbed a dry one from the rack. Wrapping it around his waist, he opened the medicine cabinet and removed his razor and inserted a new blade, the last one. "Time to get some more," he muttered, eying the empty container. "Have to remember to put 'em on the list." He hated shaving with a dull blade, which he had had to do in the past a few times when he forgot to get a new supply. After pitching the empty container into the trash, Wade lathered his face, first checking the mark left where he had hit his cheek on a stub while going down the cliff after Patty. He was right; it didn't need medical attention. It would heal just fine without all the fussing.

Covering the deep scratch with lather, he winced slightly at the sting. "Good for it," he muttered. "Kill any remaining germs." The paramedic had given it a quick clean but recommended stitches. Wade had declined. Shaving completed, albeit a bit carefully in certain places, he rinsed and replaced the razor and washed the remaining lather from his face and dried with the towel that he removed from his waist before pitching it into the towel rack. Then forgetting about his injury, Wade grabbed his aftershave lotion and splashed it on generously and nearly came up off the floor when it hit his cut. Fanning his face to help the sting, he thought wryly, *If any germs are still alive, they have to be super germs.*

Looking closely at the cut, he grabbed the tube of antibiotic salve and dabbed it on and covered it with a Band-Aid to keep it clean.

Fishing into the bureau for underwear, Wade was unimpressed with the bronze statue perfection that his perfectly tuned body made, as reflected in the mirror. As long as he felt good and had plenty of energy, he was happy.

Unbeknownst to Wade, when he was introduced to Wilma for the first time when she went to work at the station six months after she lost her husband, she had been tongue-tied for a few seconds. *Lord have mercy!* she had thought. *That had ought to come in a plain brown wrapper!* She was, after all, fifty-six at the time, not dead. Didn't do her blood pressure any good either.

Holding up a pair of pink polka-dot boxers, Wade frowned. "Where on earth did I get these? Someone's idea of a joke, I'll bet." Putting them back into the drawer, he hesitated then grabbed them and pitched them into the trash. "No one will know anyway," he muttered. Grabbing a pair of briefs and a T-shirt, he shoved the drawer shut and, pulling them on, went to the closet for a clean uniform.

This promised to be a busy day. He took turns with the other rangers in policing the campers, watching for badly built campfires, littering, drinking to excess; answering questions; passing out literature; making sure gates were closed; and generally protecting the wildlife, sensitive ecology, and the campers from each other. The campers were numerous as the camping season was coming to a close, and it would soon be too cold for it. The cool days and chilly nights made a campfire feel wonderful. The trees were getting their fall colors, and that alone increased the sightseers and hikers out to see the sights.

"Can't blame them for that," he said looking out the window at the contrasting colors of the golden hickory leaves, the deep-red sumac, and the evergreens against the deep-blue sky as he finished his morning coffee. Putting the cup in the sink with his plate, he grabbed his hat and stopped, did an about-face, and, fishing the empty razor blade container out of the trash, placed it on the counter as a reminder to get a fresh supply. Putting his hat on, he left to start his workday. Taking a deep appreciative breath of the invigorating air, he headed for the ranger station.

It hadn't been as bad as it might have been, he reflected that evening as he headed back to the ranger station, glancing appreciatively at the red-and-orange sunset. Everyone, for the most part, was obeying the rules, and all seemed to be having a great time. The last camp he had checked had two people in their late thirties or early forties and eleven children ranging from sixteen- to a five-year-old. This included two sets of twins, with two beagle pups thrown in. Loose pets were not allowed in the park, and Wade took the man aside and told him to leave them home next time or keep them on a leash.

"They're braver than I am. To go camping with that many children takes guts. Bet they'll be glad to get home." Shaking his head, he pulled the jeep into his usual parking space in front of the ranger station and turned it off. Shade met him when he opened the jeep door and got his due in petting and buddy talk before heading for his home cabin. After making his report, Wade headed for his cabin, looking forward to a hot shower and supper.

Wilma met him in front of his cabin and asked after his health. Knowing that wasn't why she was here on a Saturday, he waited for it. Finally, looking a bit red in the face, she got to the point.

"Wade, I was wondering if you found some of your underwear to be...er, a bit unusual in color?"

"You mean, like polka dots?" He grinned.

"You found them? I have yours, and if you don't mind, could we exchange them? I got them mixed the last wash I did for you, and Jer...er, the owner wants them back." Handing his white briefs to him, she waited expectantly.

Suddenly remembering just where the polka-dot shorts were, he hastily told her he would bring them right out. Going to the bedroom, he tossed his briefs on the bed and took Jerry's shorts out of the trash can and shook them out. Then folding them, he went to the door and handed them out. Thanking him, she left, and Wade mused, "So...Jerry is the owner of the pink polka-dot shorts. I'll have to remember that." Grinning, he tossed his hat at the table and headed for the shower.

Wade was just finished with his dinner and the dishes and was headed for his recliner chair with a good book when someone knocked on the door. He did an about-face, opened the door, and found the captain looking at him with a troubled face.

"Hi, Captain, what can I do for you?" Stepping aside, Wade motioned him in and shut the door.

"Wade, I'm in a fix. I need some one to take April to the church auction tomorrow afternoon. I also need to be somewhere else at the same time, so I'm afraid can't. I was wondering if I might talk you into doing it?"

"I can't either. I promised Patty I would tell her the park story again. I just might know someone who will, though. I can get Jerry to take her. They are about the same age."

Raising his eyebrows, Captain Jessup expressed his doubts that Jerry would want to be an escort to an auction, especially with April. If he remembered right, the two of them mixed like oil and water.

"I'll talk him into it," Wade assured him.

A bit irritated at Wade's cocky assurance, Jessup exclaimed, "Bet you a ten that he won't!"

"You're on, Captain, I'll see you after I go off duty tomorrow to collect."

"We'll see." Whistling, the captain left, smugly convinced that Wade didn't know about April and Jerry's incompatibility.

Wade shut the door and rubbed his hands together and, with a wicked grin, murmured, "Knowledge is power!"

The captain was still absent the next afternoon when Wade stopped at the ranger station to collect on his bet, so he turned in his report and headed home to shower before heading for Jess's cabin for a visit with Patty.

Ranger Jerry Walters had been mad as a teased tomcat but had agreed to take April to the auction. It wasn't something he was looking forward to doing but was better than the fact that he wore pink-polka dot shorts getting around. He would never live that down. His favorite nephew had given them to him for his birthday, and he had promised to wear them proudly, but he figured he had worn them enough. He had kept his promise, albeit "proudly" didn't exactly come into it, and made himself a promise right then and there. He was going to burn the blasted things first chance he got. He had to cancel a date to take April to the auction, but a man had to protect his reputation. Six-year-old children simply didn't shop for a man's shorts. Someone else was to blame for his predicament. He intended to find out who it was too.

Calling his date to cancel took only a few minutes, claiming duty priority; then he headed for the shower to get ready to take the spoiled brat to an auction. "Somebody's going to pay for this, big time!" he muttered later as he left his cabin. Meeting his canceled date at the auction didn't help one bit!

Wade peeked into the room where his small friend was recovering from her fall and smiled at her delighted expression on spotting him. Opening the door the rest of the way, he entered and handed her the daisies that he had stopped alongside the road for. They were her favorite flowers in all the world, as she would say. Putting them in an empty vase after adding water from the bathroom sink, Wade sat them where she could see them and pulled up a chair.

Ranger Wade

"How you doing, young'un?" Wade asked as settled into the rather hard chair. He grinned as he thought about the time he found Sue laughing her head off just after he said "See you later, young'un," to a four-year-old Patty. Asking what was so funny, Wade joined in when Sue told him between chuckles, "Patty said you called her an onion."

"I'm okay," Patty muttered guiltily. "I wasn't really close to the edge, Ranger Wade. The ground was slippery 'cause of the pine needles, and it was downhill, and I couldn't stop sliding. I though I was gonna die!" she blurted with tears running down her cheeks. She had known better than to play near the cliffs. A hard lesson learned, he thought.

"Well, you'll know better next time, right?" he asked gently and, after getting her nod, changed the subject.

"You 'bout ready for the park story?" he asked and grinned as her face lit up like a light, between the bruises anyway. "Okay here goes."

4

A long, long time ago, dating back over ten thousand years ago, humans left evidence behind. These people are believed to be the ancestors of the tribes that live in the area today. By the time the first European explorers came to this region, several different tribes inhabited the area. The Blackfoot Indians controlled the vast prairies east of the mountains. The Salish and Kootenai Indians lived and hunted in the western valleys. They also traveled east of the mountains to hunt buffalo.

In the early eighteen hundreds, French, English, and Spanish trappers came in search of beaver. In 1806, the Lewis and Clark Expedition came within fifty miles of the area that is now the park.

As the number of people moving west steadily increased, the Blackfeet, Salish, and Kootenai were forced on reservations. The Blackfeet Reservation adjoins the east side of the park. The Salish and Kootenai Reservation is southwest of Glacier. This entire area holds great spiritual importance to the Blackfeet, Salish, and Kootenai people.

The railroad over Marias Pass was completed in 1891. The completion of the Great Northern Railway allowed more people to enter the area. Homesteaders settled in the valleys west of Marias Pass, and soon, small towns developed.

Under pressure from miners, the mountains east of the Continental Divide were acquired in 1895 from the Blackfeet. Miners came searching for copper and gold. They hoped to strike it rich, but no large copper or gold deposits were ever located. Although the mining boom lasted only a few years, abandoned mine shafts are still found in several places in the park.

Around the turn of the century, people started to look at the land differently. Rather than just seeing the minerals they could mine or land to settle on, they started to recognize the value of its spectacular, scenic beauty. Facilities for tourists started to spring up. In the late 1890s, visitors arriving at Belton (now called West Glacier) could get off the train, take a stagecoach ride for a few miles to Lake McDonald, and then board a boat for an eight-mile trip to the Snyder Hotel. No roads existed in the mountains, but the lakes allowed boat travel into the wilderness.

Soon, people, like George Bird Grinnell, pushed for the creation of a national park. Grinnell was an early explorer to this part of Montana and spent many years working to get the park established. The area was made a forest preserve in 1900 but was open to mining and homesteading. Grinnell and others sought the added protection a national park provided.

Grinnell saw his efforts rewarded in 1910 when President Taft signed the bill establishing Glacier as the country's tenth national park.

After the creation of the park, the growing staff of park rangers needed housing and offices to help protect the new park. The increasing number of park visitors made the need for roads, trails, and hotels urgent. The Great Northern Railway built a series of hotels and small backcountry lodges, called chalets, throughout the park. A typical visit to Glacier involved a train ride to the park followed by a multiday journey on horseback. Each day after a long ride in the mountains, guests would stay at a different hotel or chalet. The lack of roads meant that, to see the interior of the park, visitors had to hike or ride a horse. Eventually, the demand for a road across the mountains led to the building of the Going-to-the-Sun Road.

The construction of the Going-to-the-Sun Road was a huge undertaking. Even today, visitors to the park marvel at how such a road could have been built. The final section of the Going-to-the-Sun Road, over Logan Pass, was completed in 1932 after eleven years of work. The road is considered an engineering feat and is a National Historic Landmark. It is one of the most scenic roads in North America. The construction of the road forever changed the way visitors would experience Glacier National Park. Future visitors would drive over sections of the park that previously had taken days of horseback riding to see.

Just across the border, in Canada, is Waterton Lakes National Park. In 1931, the members of the Rotary Clubs of Alberta and Montana suggested joining the two parks as a symbol of the peace and friendship between our two countries. In 1932, the United States and Canadian governments voted to designate the parks as Waterton-Glacier International Peace Park, the world's first. More recently, the parks have received two other international honors. The parks are both biosphere reserves and were named as a World Heritage site in 1995. This international recognition highlights the importance of this area—not just to the United States and Canada but to the entire world. While much has changed since the first visitors came to Glacier, it is possible to relive some of Glacier's early history. You can take a horseback ride like an early visitor. Miles of hiking trails follow routes first used by trappers in the early 1800s. Several hotels and chalets, built by the Great Northern Railway in the early 1900s, house summer guests to the park. A visit to Glacier National Park is still a great adventure.[1]

Putting down his notes and info sheets, Wade looked at his listener and smiled as he realized that she was still dreamily living in the history that he had just read to her. Never had he seen such love for the wilderness as this precocious child has. She would indeed make a heck of a park ranger.

1. National Park Service, US Department of the Interior

Clearing his throat, Wade brought Patty back to the present. Looking at him a little startled, she grinned and held out her one good arm for a hug. "Thank you so much, Ranger Wade, I love to hear this kind of history. I wished I was borned a hundred years ago so I could be there instead of hearing about it."

Grinning, Wade replied, "A hundred years from now, they will be wishing they were born right about now so they could live in your lifetime instead of hearing about it. Love what you have instead of what's gone and help save it for the ones that come after you are gone."

"Okay. Rangers do that, don't they?" Patty said with a yawn.

"They sure do," Wade agreed, and taking the hint, notwithstanding the nurse that was frowning at him from the door, Wade rose and kissed his little friend good-bye. "You need to get your rest so you can hurry and come home. See you later, alligator," he quipped.

"After…while…"

Wade picked up his hat from the foot of the bed and, looking back at the sleeping child, thanked God again that she had been spared. Her loss would have left a very big hole in a lot of lives.

The nurse wasn't looking so forbidding now that he was leaving, and Wade gave her a grin as he left. He didn't see her smile a bit wistfully in return; his infectious grin was hard to ignore.

5

"You sure you want to come? It is your day off," Wade asked Jess as he threw the cooler into the back of the jeep. "Might take a while to catch him. I only know approximately when he does the dynamiting. It's about every three days, and today's the third day."

"Better than a cabin full of complaining females," Jess grumbled. "I shudder to think of spending all day at home nowadays. Sure be glad when things get back to normal."

"Hey, you asked for it when you invited your sister-in-law to convalesce at your house. Hang in there. It can't last forever."

"Feels like it already has, but right about then, I would have agreed to anything to bring a smile back to Sue's face," Jess said as he climbed in the passenger's side and slammed the door.

"Take it easy on my door. I already had to replace one this year," Wade admonished his friend as they pulled away from the ranger station.

"That wasn't from getting slammed. You got in the way of a charging moose cow." Jess grinned, his humor restored.

"Oh, shut up," Wade muttered, and their combined laughter floated back as they disappeared into the forest.

Forty minutes later, Wade pulled into a thick stand of young pines about a quarter mile from the lakeshore. It was just after sunrise, and the night chill was still hanging close to the forest floor. The birds were still sounding off, and the mist from the lake was starting to move with the rising sun.

Getting closer to the lake proved to be easy with the plentiful cover. "This is as good a place as any," Wade muttered as he surveyed his surroundings. The cedar thicket had a clear center that hid them from view from anyone on or near the lake. Still, by parting the branches, they could see well enough to identify the culprit should he appear. Suddenly, Wade gave an exclamation and started to leave the circle.

"Where you going?" Jess whispered loudly.

"I forgot to turn the jeep radio off," Wade said with disgust. "If it sounds off at the wrong time, it will blow our cover."

"I'll do that if you finish setting up here." After getting Wade's nod, he whispered, "be back in a minute." And he slipped into the forest.

Jess had been gone about fifteen minutes when Wade nearly jumped out of his boots at the muffled boom of dynamite going off underwater.

Parting the cedars, he found a wooden rowboat about fifty feet out from the shore, and its occupant was watching the lake surface intently. Suddenly, he grabbed a catch net and started scooping the struggling half-stunned fish from the water. He lifted the lid of a large cooler and dumped the fish in and went after more. Twice more he made his catch; and when the effects of the dynamite have worn off, he failed to find any more on the surface. Feeling content after checking the coolers, he shrugged and closed the lid. Picking up his oars, he started rowing back to shore.

"Arnold Webb, as I live and breathe. I could have sworn he was on the straight and narrow. Never knew him to break the law before. Better see what he has to say for himself." Wade left the thicket and was waiting behind Arnold when he lifted the cooler from the boat and turned around. He nearly dropped the cooler when Wade drawled, "Well, well, if it isn't Arnold Detonator. How you doing, Arnie? Long time no see." Wade stood looking grimly at the shocked culprit.

Looking wildly around, Arnold looked like he could bolt any second; but suddenly, the starch went out of him, and he seemed to wilt. Setting the cooler on the ground, he raised his hands and waited for whatever was to come.

"You armed Arnie?" Wade asked the despondent man.

"No," was the response.

"Then you can put your hands down." Opening the cooler, Wade whistled at the size of some of the fish. "I can see why you do your fishing this way if you get very many this size, but you know it's against the law, don't you?"

Nodding, Arnold sat on a stump and waited to see what the next step would be to being put in jail. He had never been in jail before. The very thought scared him.

Closing the cooler, Wade sat on it and, looking at Arnold, said, "I'm waiting."

"Waiting…? For what?

"Your explanation. Why are you dynamiting fish when it's perfectly legal to fish in this lake the right way? You can't be that lazy. Or are you just in that much of a hurry?"

Scrubbing his hand through his hair, Arnold muttered, "You got a few minutes? I'll tell you."

"I'm all ears," Wade assured him.

"Well, about two years ago, Willow started acting funny, seeing things that wasn't there, running away from home, scared of things that she didn't used to be scared of, like squirrels and rabbits, the dark—things like that. I took off work and took her to the city to one of them fancy doctors, and after they had most of my savings, they said that she had a tumor in her brain. Not operable.

"I had to quit my job to take care of her, and after a while, we didn't have any more money for food and the like. We been living off fish and wild greens now for about four months. When she takes her nap—which she always does in the morning after being up most of the night—I book it to the lake and stock up on fish the quickest way I can so I can maybe get some sleep before she wakes up. Last time I took her in, Doc said she would be gone in a couple of months, but that's been almost four months ago, and she's still hanging in there. I figured to stay with her long as she needed me." Looking at Wade with the beginning of panic in his eyes, he whispered, "What's she going to do with me in jail? Who's gonna take care of her?"

Stunned, Wade stared at Arnold. He was prepared to take a criminal to jail and found instead a man hurting something fierce and desperately needing help. Shaking his head, Wade stood and, taking Arnold's arm, helped him to stand also, noting that he was shaking with stress and had lost a lot of weight since the last time he had seen him.

"Arnie, I want you to take the fish home, and you needn't worry about going to jail. There are people who help with situations like yours. You go on home and take care of Willow, and I'll send someone around to talk to you about that help, okay?"

With tears in his eyes, Arnold nodded, too choked to speak, and, grabbing Wade's hand, shook it hard. Grabbing the cooler, he tore through the brush in his hurry to get back to Willow.

Wade had just made it back to their observation point and started packing when a loud crashing from the cedar thicket startled Wade, and he turned in time to see Jess stumble into the clearing and stand staring at him. "Well?"

"Well what?"

"Did you catch him? The dynamiter? I heard a thump like dynamite going off underwater, you had to have heard it. Didn't you?"

"Jess, where you been?" Wade shot back at Jess, ignoring the question.

Opening his mouth then closing it and swallowing, Jess muttered, "Up a tree."

"What were you doing up a tree? We had serious business to tend to here, and you're horsing around?"

Forgetting the unanswered question, which was Wade's intention, Jess swallowed again and stated that he wasn't horsing around; he had returned to the jeep to turn off the radio and found a grizzly bear messing with it. He threw a stick at it, and it promptly came for him. He simply went up the nearest tree big enough to climb. He had turned off the radio and rejoined Wade as soon as the bear left. "What happened here?" he added.

"We aren't going to catch anyone after all that racket and activity," Wade said mournfully. "Guess we might as well pack it in and head back to the ranger station." Watching Jess from the corner of his eye, Wade was relieved when Jess agreed and started gathering equipment. He hid a grin when Jess muttered something about a sonic boom.

6

Pulling into the parking spot in front of Jess's cabin, Wade shut the motor off and pushed the jeep's door open, with a bit of difficulty as Shade was trying to climb in at the same time. "Back, Shade," Wade spoke sternly and made his exit with the foot that Shade allowed him. Shutting the door, Wade gave him the "buddy" talk and a good petting that he expected from his friend. Shade was a very large dog and needed a lot of exercise and that had been curtailed quite a bit when Patty returned from the hospital. Shade insisted on spending as much time as possible by her side and only left her when he had to. Satisfied with the attention that he received from his friend, Shade bolted for the woods for the badly needed exercise. After watching him for a few seconds, Wade knocked on Jess's door. Patty looked forward to his visits so much that he simply couldn't resist seeing her every chance he got.

"Ranger Wade, is that you?" Patty yelled from the living room couch.

"Patty, hush, you'll wake your Aunt Peggy. Hello, Wade, she hasn't talked about anything else since she found out you were coming. Perhaps now my ears can have a rest. There's coffee if you want some."

"No, thanks," Wade said as he sailed his hat at the rack of antlers over the fireplace. It caught a point and spun twice then hung there like he hoped it would. It really impressed Patty when he did that. Big-eyed, she scooted over so he could sit beside her. "You going to tell me what all the rangers do, Ranger Wade? I know I'm going to be a ranger, but I don't know which kind yet."

Grinning, Wade lifted the folded sheets of paper from his shirt pocket and sat beside her. "Okay, Miss Ranger-to-be, here goes." Looking down at Patty when she snuggled against him, he smiled and turned to the informational pages he had used for this same purpose twice before.

A park ranger (then called a forest ranger) is a person charged with protecting and preserving protected park lands, forests, wilderness areas as well as other natural resources and protected cultural resources. Some countries use the term "park warden" to describe this occupation. The profession has often been oversimply characterized as "protecting the people from the resource and the resource from the people." The profession includes a number of disciplines and specializations, and park rangers in the United States and elsewhere are often required to be proficient in more than one. For example, the mission of "protection and preservation" is also to be achieved by rangers who interpret the resources to the public in order to encourage their stewardship—not simply only demanding compliance through law enforcement.

There are 390 units in the US National Park system with over a dozen different designations, including such titles as national monument, national seashore, national park, national historic site, national preserve, national wilderness area, and national recreation area.

Internationally, many countries have conservation agencies that undertake the protection and management of natural areas and protected culture areas. The park rangers within these organizations are represented at this international level by the International Ranger Federation.

Park rangers perform a number of important functions in the protection of wildlands. In isolated areas many miles from inhabited regions, park rangers may be the only "official" presence…if not the only person around. Because they are the only persons around, park rangers must be very conscious of safety issues; they may respond very differently from other emergency responders who have assistance close by.

Park rangers perform a diverse number of other tasks; these tasks range from routine maintenance to life-saving emergency response and search and rescue.

Skills often required in being a park ranger include a profound interest in ecology and the wilderness, the ability to react quickly and appropriately to emergency situations, and the ability to work independently and alone for long periods…sometimes for many days in a row.

Glancing at Patty, Wade found her to be wide awake and absorbing everything like a sponge. Wryly, Wade thought he wasn't going to be able to cut it short this time, like in the hospital when her medication became too much for her to fight, allowing him to escape with dignity.

Grinning, Wade began again.

Duties, disciplines, and specializations. There are various park ranger disciplines, and not every park ranger will perform all of them. An interpretation ranger—responsible for an array of visitor services, tours, information exhibits, etc.— has different primary duties than a law enforcement ranger. Many rangers, however, must be relied upon to be competent in functions beyond their primary duties. For example, a ranger with just primary law enforcement duties may also provide interpretive programming, so may a ranger with primary interpretation duties be trained and serve as a wildland firefighter. Only certified, "commissioned," park rangers may perform law enforcement duties, however, just as wildland firefighters is only authorized for properly trained and certified personnel duties. The field of interpretation is becoming increasingly professionalized as well, as colleges and universities in greater numbers are offering degrees in the field and certification becomes more common. Within the structure of a unit of the US National Park system, there are often various divisions. These sometimes include law enforcement, resources management, interpretation, maintenance, and administration. Park rangers may be found in any of these divisions but are most often associated with the first three.

"Uh…Ranger Wade?"

"Yes, Patty?"

"Could we not do that part and go to the part where it tells what's in the jeep?"

"Sure we can…let's see, here we are. This part is called… vehicle and equipment."

"Yeah…that the one!" Patty said and snuggled into Wade's side a bit more and relaxed and waited for him to start again.

A typical ranger vehicle is a well-marked and heavily equipped off-road-capable light truck (pickup truck)—often equipped with the following items (the variety of equipment carried gives some idea of the many roles of the park ranger):

- A reliable radio or mobile telephone, often with a backup device for emergencies
- An electronic locator unit such as a GPS, in remote areas supplemented by an EPIRB for signaling for help
- Detailed maps of the area protected and guidebooks about local flora and fauna
- A clipboard and paperwork used to document activities, including a daily patrol report, citation book, incident report, and maintenance reports
- Informational handouts and maps to be given to visitors
- A collection of keys that open gates, locks, and buildings scattered across the park or preserve
- Personal survival equipment for an extended stay in the wilderness, including a backpack, tent, and sleeping bag as well as fire-starting equipment
- A comprehensive first aid kit including supplies for response to trauma and vehicle accidents
- Personal flashlight, folding pocket knife, multi tool, handcuffs, chemical defense spray, defensive baton
- Blankets, emergency food and water, and portable tarps or other shelter (for any persons rescued)
- Hand tools including a shovel, ax, rake, Pulaski tool, crowbar, bolt cutter, and other miscellaneous tools
- A power winch for extricating stuck vehicles, with associated cables
- Rope and life preserver for unassisted water rescue
- Handheld fire extinguishers, a backpack fire pump, a one-inch (25 mm) diameter 50-foot (15 m) length of

fire hose with a 50 to 150 US gallon (200 to 600L) firewater tank and gasoline-powered reversible pump, fireproof turnout coat, and a self-rescue fire shelter
- Firearms, if appropriate to the area, often including a high-powered rifle with optical sights and a pump-action shotgun for close-range defense (park rangers engaged in police activities will often carry a pistol at all times in addition)
- Additional supplies of fuel and water as appropriate

These supplies are often augmented according to the geographic area and the local hazards. A park ranger in urban areas may carry less survival gear and more law enforcement equipment; a park ranger in the desert will carry much more drinking water; a park ranger in the Alaskan outback will carry additional shelter materials and stove fuel. In more remote areas, prepositioned catches containing survival equipment will be scattered throughout the park.[1]

"The end. Do you think you'll remember all that?" Wade asked as he folded his informational packet.

A small snore was the only response. Grinning, Wade eased away from the sleeping child and, being careful of her casts, straightened her on the couch and covered her with the ready blanket. Sue was catching up on things in the kitchen

---

1. *Wikipedia: The Free Encyclopedia*

while Patty was occupied. Inactivity was not something Patty was good at and she kept her mother running for things she really didn't need or even want out of sheer boredom.

"Out like a light," Wade commented as he grabbed a muffin from the plate on the table.

"Wade, those are for the church charity sale. God will get you for that." Sue smiled as she poured him a cup of coffee to go with it."

"God would understand that one works up a real appetite keeping Patty occupied," Wade came back through his muffin-filled mouth.

Chuckling, Sue placed another muffin on a saucer in front of Wade and discreetly put the rest away. Sitting in the chair across from him with her own cup of coffee, Sue waited patiently for him to finish off the muffins.

Sitting back in the chair, Wade sighed. "Thanks, I needed that. Didn't have time for supper this evening."

"Oh Wade, why didn't you say something, I have plenty of leftovers in the fridge."

"That's all right, the muffins took the edge off. I'll last till morning," he said, reaching for his hat.

"You just wait a minute, Sergeant Wade McKenna. I'll make you a meatloaf sandwich to take with you. It's the least I can do after you babysat Patty for the last couple of hours and let me catch up on things. That child is a real trial when she's pinned down like this."

Wade thanked Sue for the sandwich and, stooping to pet the large orange tomcat on his way out, left for his cabin and waiting bed. He made it halfway to his cabin when the smell of the sandwich got to him. By the time he entered his front door, he had half the sandwich gone and needed something to drink with it.

Meatloaf on homemade bread just couldn't be resisted, he thought as he took a carton of milk out of the refrigerator. He figured he could live on nothing but that for at least a month without complaining a bit. Well, a couple of weeks anyway, he thought.

Yawning, Wade threw the empty milk carton in the trash and added milk to his shopping list. "Better get some bread too. That homemade bread that Sue makes could spoil a man. Wonder if I could get her to make me some…better not." He added regretfully, "She has enough to do right now, maybe later." Yawning again, he headed for bed, but made a U-turn and added razor blades to the list. Stripping to his briefs, he climbed in and pulled the cover up. It had been a long day. *Might check on Arnie tomorrow and see how he's doing*, he thought just before sleep took him.

7

Having woken early, Wade lay in bed for a while longer, enjoying the relaxed feel of a bit more time before he had to get up and get ready for another day.

The catbird outside his window that had awakened him brought back memories of his own childhood. One of the numerous pets he and his siblings had was a large tomcat that could have been the double of his partner's.

The wilderness was their playground, a good deal like Patty. But boys doing that caused little or no concern where a girl caused uneasiness, even more so since her accident, he thought.

They tackled anything together, even a huge blacksnake longer than they were. Having killed it, they took it home to proudly show their parents and sisters, much to their sister's consternation. Their father sat them down and explained the blacksnakes' place in the ecology of things—getting rid of rats, mice and even poison snakes. Giving their promise not to harm any more blacksnakes, they were told to take it out and bury it. A bit crestfallen and feeling a bit deflated, they decided to have a bit of fun and regain some self-esteem. Placing the snake in a straight line, they picked up the tomcat and held him over the snake and dropped him.

The cat saw the snake about the time he landed astraddle of it, and in a blind panic, he convulsively leaped, straight up, and consequently landed on the snake again, eliciting another prodigious leap—this time fortunately sideways—and digging in with ears flattened against his head and tail twice it's normal size. He had made tracks for the woods.

The boys fell over themselves cracking up, not seeing their father frowning past his grin. The cat wandered back into the yard rather cautiously about an hour later and started for his water dish on the back porch. It was unfortunate that he happened to cross the rope about the time Wade gave it a yank, and the cat, still a bit rattled, went airborne once more. He was gone for the rest of the day this time.

Grinning at the memory, Wade admitted to himself that they had been a bit ornery when they were growing up, but they hadn't really hurt anything—except for the snake, that is. He threw back the covers and sat up in bed.

What one of his three brothers and two sisters couldn't think of, another one could. Growing up hadn't been dull, that was for sure, he thought as he headed for the shower. A bit later, digging into his drawer for clean briefs, he thought again about the pink polka-dot shorts and, grinning, wondered how Jerry's date with the captain's niece had gone.

Which reminded him—he hadn't collected his bet from the captain yet. He hoped the captain never found out the method of persuasion that he used on Jerry. He imagined that the captain would certainly frown on blackmail of any kind, even if it was funny. Grinning, Wade grabbed his hat and headed for the ranger station, knowing that Wilma would have doughnuts and coffee ready.

Stomping his boots to shake off the snow, Wade entered the ranger station and looked around as he removed his down-filled parka and gloves. His hat got a shaking also, and he sailed it toward the antler rack on the wall. It caught a tine and, after a couple of circles, settled.

"I'm waiting for you to miss when you do that. The law of averages says that eventually, you will," the captain muttered as he sat a cup of coffee on his desk and took a seat in the swivel chair behind it. "This weather has decided to get serious, radio says at least a foot of snow and it's going to drop to near zero tonight. Sure glad camping season's over. We'd have a hard time rescuing anyone caught out in this. Only been over for two weeks—cut it a bit close, I think. We should end it middle of September instead of the end. Better safe than sorry."

Listening to the forlorn sound of Wilma's wind chimes in the snow-laden wind as he poured his coffee, Wade silently agreed. Grabbing a couple of the doughnuts from an open box, he went to the window and watched the heavily falling snow as he munched his instant breakfast. He brought up another possible problem. "Time to get ready for poachers taking advantage of yarded elk and such."

"Just about. How's Patty and Peggy doing?" the captain asked as he joined Wade at the window.

Glancing at him, Wade grinned. "Peggy is still moving slow, but she's moving without help now. Patty has a walking cast, and it isn't slowing her down much. This snow will help keep her inside where she should be." He added more to himself, "I hope."

Grinning at Wade, the captain said thoughtfully, "I hope I'm still around when she makes ranger. She's going to be something else. Just what, well…we'll have to wait and see, I guess." Shaking his head, he returned to his desk and started through papers that had needed his attention for some time. "Look at this. Hope he's headed in the other direction. We certainly don't need his kind around here." Frowning, the captain handed Wade a circular.

Wade turned the paper around, and his eyes went cold and deadly. "When did he escape?" The man looking at him from the page was one he knew well. Wade was responsible for putting him in prison—for life, he thought. Scott Karnes: professional poacher who took the life of a ranger. When he was confronted with it, he ran, and Wade made it his business to track him down. The man was smart, Wade admitted, but not too smart or he should have been making a living doing something honest.

Jeannie Murnette Smith

The ranger that Karnes killed had been Wade's partner, and Wade stayed on his trail for nearly five months until he finally ran him down in his hometown in a rural area of Kansas. The tornado that hit his hometown didn't do it any good, and the news camera had caught a good likeness of Karnes in passing as it covered the tornado-ravaged town. Wade had him before he knew he was in the vicinity. With the local law as backup, he soon had his prisoner in jail and then on his way back to Montana to face first-degree murder plus poaching and as many other charges as Wade could throw at him. He came back to the present when the captain spoke again.

"This came with it. He disappeared from a work gang about a week ago. One of the prisoners was injured in an accident, and he took advantage of the distraction." The captain handed Wade the second paper and waited.

"The warden suspects that he will head back here. Says that while he was in, all he wanted to talk about was getting even with the ranger that took away his freedom. Devised all kinds of ways to do that too, and he says that some of them were pretty scary. I take it you know this man?"

"Yeah, I know him," Wade muttered. "He killed my last partner when he tried to take him for poaching. It took me over five months to catch him. It happened about a year before you took Captain Philipps's place when he retired." Wade, frowning and looking grimmer than ever, muttered, "Think he would hurt my friends to get at me? I wouldn't put it past him. He stopped drawing the line a long time ago, and

I honestly don't think he's sane." Throwing the paper back on the captain's desk, Wade grabbed his jacket and hat and left the station and headed over to the Beals to see Patty and warn Jess about a possible visit from the escaped con. He intended to wear his gun at all times from now on, at least until Scott Karnes was captured again. He would warn Jess and the other rangers under him to do the same. If Karnes hurts another ranger, he would kill him this time, Wade thought grimly.

The snow was a good six inches deep already and showed no sign of abating. It was coming down even thicker, if anything, Wade thought as he cleaned the snow off his boots on his partner's porch. Could get more than the predicted foot, easily.

He knocked on the door at the same time Jess was opening it, and he almost knocked for an invitation on his partner's face. A quick ducking motion took care of the problem, and with a grin, Jess invited him in. Wade grinned as he recognized the quick *clunk, pat, clunk, pat* sound of Patty and her walking cast and bare foot.

"What are you going to read to me this time, Ranger Wade?" Patty asked breathlessly as she hurried up to Wade and looked expectantly at him.

"This is official business this time, young'un. No time for that right now. Maybe later, okay?" He regretted the disappointment on her face, but it couldn't be helped. Being seated at the table with milk and cookies seemed to appeased her, at least for the time being, Wade thought.

"We need to talk," Wade said, looking meaningfully at Jess.

"Okay, I wanted to show you my new snowshoes anyway. Made by a professional, expensive too, but worth it." Jess led the way into the bedroom and closed the door. Rounding on Wade, he waited for him to say what was bothering him. Something was for sure, something serious.

Twenty minutes later, Jess and Wade left the bedroom, and Jess told Sue that they were going over to the ranger station for a bit.

Stomping off the snow, they entered the station, and Wade went to the captain's desk and picked up the wanted poster of Karnes. Handing it to Jess, he said, "Remember what he looks like. He's armed and dangerous. This man is the one that killed my last partner. I don't want to lose another one. From now on, all park rangers will carry side arms. Patrol in pairs and carry a radio. He's out for revenge and could very well use my friends to get to me. I don't think he's sane. Whatever you do, do not trust him. He's treacherous. Lock up the house at night, and when you are gone. Keep all out buildings locked. You need to warn Sue, and you might think about sending your family and sister-in-law to your sister-in-law's place for a while till we can get a handle on this. Sue can take care of them there just as well, and it would free you to concentrate on things without worrying that he might get to one of them.

If you see him, don't try to take him by yourself…Call for backup and watch him till it arrives, understood?"

"Understood, and Wade…I've never seen you spooked before. He must be something else," Jess replied as they headed back to Jess's cabin.

"He is," Wade growled. "He's half-French, half-Indian of some kind, six foot one, two hundred solid pounds of pure mean and one hundred percent treacherous. Like I said, don't trust him!"

Leaving Jess at his door, Wade headed back to his own cabin to make some calls. He wanted all the information he could about the situation, plus any updates on Karnes's whereabouts that were available.

"Yeah, he's something else, all right," Wade muttered to himself as he trudged through the snow to his cabin "And if he touches one of my friends, I'll hand him his head on a platter!" he finished savagely.

The back of his neck prickled…that was a forerunner of trouble! It always was. Rubbing it, Wade carefully checked his surroundings without being obvious about it. Still checking as he kicked the snow off his boots on his front porch, he unlocked the door and slipped inside. Cracking the door, he watched for a while and grunted in frustration. The situation was making him paranoid. Throwing his hat at the antler rack, he stared at it as it bounced off the wall above the rack and hit the floor.

"The man has me plum rattled," he muttered as he retrieved the hat and put it on the rack. *The captain would agree too*, he thought wryly as he shrugged out of his parka. "Glad he didn't see that. It would have made his day!"

It was his turn to check the yarded elk and cruise his area, checking for anything out of the ordinary. They yarded with the first heavy snow, and that was a fact already. Watching the snow fall was usually a peaceful experience. It brought back memories of his childhood. His youngest sibling was only four and his oldest twelve when their parents were killed in an avalanche along with two other couples on their honeymoon. He, himself, had just turned fourteen. It took two days to find them all. In the meantime, having been notified of the death of their only son and his wife, Wade's grandparents quickly came after them and took all six home with them.

His grandparents owned a huge ranch that had been left to his grandfather by his grandfather. His great-great-grandfather had been raised in abject poverty. He had determinedly searched for the mother lode among the gold miners of California and had, by sheer chance, hit pay dirt. He had climbed a small tree to get away from a grizzly bear with cubs, which he had come on unexpectedly with nearly disastrous results. The tree was just large enough to keep him out of her reach, and when she finally left, he started to descend. But the tree, weakened by her battering in her efforts to reach him, simply fell over, taking him with it.

Ranger Wade

Half-stunned, he picked himself up and attempted to brush off the dirt, staring at the uprooted small tree while thanking God that it held until the bear gave up and left. Then he realized that he was looking at something that glittered. Checking it out, he found the gold in his future mine, which he called Bear Load. It didn't make him rich but gave him the start he needed. And by investing and sheer determination, he was on his way to being rich. He strove relentlessly to achieve the top, and when he finally found himself there, he found it empty—nothing meaningful there. It was then that he realized that what he was searching for was among that which he had left behind in his zeal to reach the top. He was too late to undo the harm that he had done to an abandoned wife and son. So he did liquidate everything that he owned and headed for Montana and searched until he found the huge track of land that met his requirements—water, timber, type of grass and the general lay of the land, plus never having been flooded. Buying it, he built a huge ranch house, barns, bunk houses, corrals and fenced in the thousand-acre lot of it. Satisfied, he stocked it with cattle, the best stock horses—mostly a Morgan cross—and hiring the necessary people to run it for him. Then he went in search of his grandson that the private investigators had found for him.

By this time, he was dying from overwork, stress, and a cancer that was slowly getting to him. He also made a will, leaving everything to his grandson, Wade's grandfather, Wade McKenna—whom Wade had been named after. His grandson was civil to him but was still pretty much estranged when he died. Taking possession left the elder Wade feeling bad for the way he had treated his grandfather. He didn't know his grandfather was dying when he made contact.

The large ranch was now a complex operation, raising a multitude of animals for breeding, meat, and to sell. The size of the ranch allowed them to raise most of the feed needed, and everyone was too busy to feel sorry for themselves. It turned out to be good therapy.

When his youngest brother was off to college, Wade packed, kissed his grandma, and left to join the rangers, having completed his own college courses some time ago. He was after hands-on experience now. His grandfather was gone after two strokes, one after another, and he hated to leave his grandmother alone, but she insisted that he "do his thing."

He grinned at her memory. She was the scrappiest woman he had ever known for her size, bar none. Five foot five, lean as a whip, and never still, she had grown up whipping boys that picked on her handicapped brother. She had still enjoyed a good scrap now and again at sixty-nine, although they were all verbal by then.

Grinning even wider, Wade let the memories come of the time when he'd had to go to the city on ranger business and she found out about his impending trip and talked him into taking her with him. It had been fun to see her wide-eyed wonder at the tall buildings and the people living practically on top of each other. She loved the peace and quiet of country living and couldn't understand why they chose to live like this. The crowds frayed her nerves, and by the time he was ready to head home, she was very glad to leave the city. Showing her the park fountains on the last day before heading home, he went to a food stand to buy her some flavored ice. He turned back in time to see her deck a rough-looking man twice her size. The man sat up and looked at her in amazement and opened his mouth to tell her off when she raised her eyebrow without saying a word. He snapped his mouth shut and, after glancing at Wade, scrambled to his feet and took off down the path. Wade watched in amazement.

"Grams, what happened, did he insult you? Why did you hit him?"

Picking her purse off the park bench where she put it to free her hands, she said with satisfaction, "He asked me to."

"He asked you to hit him?"

"Yep, he sure did," she responded, and taking a bite of the flavored ice, she grinned. "He don't speak our language I guess," she said around a mouthful of the flavorful confection.

"That's no reason to hit him!"

"That's not why I hit him. He said a few words I didn't understand. When I asked him what, he kind of snarled, 'Want smack!' So I gave him one."

Wade groaned, "Grams, smack is another name for dope. The man must be addicted and he was trying to get a fix. If I hadn't been close by, he could have killed you."

"Don't see what all the fuss is about. I fixed him didn't I?" she snorted and returned her attention to the melting cone. Cherry was her favorite flavor.

Eyeing her for a few seconds, Wade made up his mind right there that he would never put her in that kind of danger again. The fact that he had on his uniform might have helped deter the man, but he wasn't taking any chances.

"Time to head home," he said firmly, and they proceeded to do just that.

8

A few years later, he lost his grams to a mean bull. Two cows had been brought to the ranch for servicing to the sixty-thousand-dollar bull; the health certificates were not with them. They were placed in the pen next to the bull until the health certificates caught up with them. Three days of frustration at being unable to reach the cows had put the bull in a nasty frame of mind. When the papers came through, Gram's men were afraid to handle him, so she tackled him herself, having had no trouble with him before, and was in the pen before any was aware of her intentions. Wade had arrived to see the men all gathered around the bull pen and found her still lying on the ground in the pen, torn and bleeding. Wade had pulled his side arm and shot the sixty-thousand-dollar bull between the eyes.

Gathering her frail body in his arms, he told the foreman to call 911 and started blindly for the house. It was the only time that his men would ever see him cry.

Lord, he missed that scrappy little woman! She had filled a big hole in his and his siblings' lives. The ranch had been left to the six grandchildren, and it still operated under a manager. He hadn't gone back much since then. He would have to check and see how things were going one day. Losing Grams left him with a big hole in his heart that the ranch seemed to remind him of.

Returning to the present, Wade checked outside again and turned on the kitchen light. It was not quite time for supper yet, but he needed something to do.

First, though, he called everyone in the vicinity and clued them in on the escaped con and the possibility that he was headed in this direction. His last call was to Jess to see if he had talked his family into staying at his sister-in-law's home until they could sort this problem out. He breathed a sigh of relief when Jess told him they had reluctantly agreed. Sue was packing as they spoke. Wade cautioned Jess not to say anything to anyone about the move and put the luggage in the trunk after full dark, using no lights. The last thing he wanted was an ambush with them all being held hostage at once. Hanging up the phone, Wade started for the kitchen to prepare supper. A sandwich would do; he wasn't very hungry. His appetite could improve if he had some of Sue's homemade bread to make sandwich with, he thought wistfully.

Turning out the lights after he finished, Wade stood at the bedroom window and watched the snow fall for a while. It was soothing in the large yard light that lit the ranger station and the area around it. It looked a bit lighter than earlier; maybe it was letting up. He hoped so. It could complicate recapturing Karnes if it got much deeper.

Well, worry about that tomorrow, he thought wearily. Dropping the curtains, he stripped to his briefs and crawled under the covers.

Wade dreamed of his life with Grams and Grandpa. His grandpa had been a bit of a rascal, and had actually made his own moonshine. Grams wouldn't have anything to do with it. "Too full of surprises," she declared. Two of Grandpa's friends had played cards with him one evening when Wade was still home and everything was fine until they rose to leave. Then they simply started swinging at each other. Grams and Grandpa guided the struggling pair outside and let them have it out. When they quit and snores started, Grams threw a blanket over the pair and let them sleep it off. They left the next morning leaning on each other and walking on eggs.

Grams liked the home brew that she made and so did a lot of her neighbors and friends. Then one day, the sheriff pulled up in his Model A and announced that making moonshine was against the law. He told Grandpa that he was under arrest.

Now Grandpa didn't lose his cool; he simply asked the sheriff if he could take the wagon to town and load it with groceries for the old woman and the kids as he would be awhile getting home again. Now the sheriff liked grams's home brew as much as anyone else did, so he said that he would wait here for grandpa to get back with the groceries. He settled in with a mug of the brew and watched grandpa out of sight.

In about an hour or a bit more, the wagon came home loaded with the promised groceries, and the seat was empty. The old mare headed home; she didn't need to be guided. The sheriff threw a fit but couldn't do anything about it. After he left, Grams poured herself a brew and sipped it, chuckling to herself every little bit while putting the groceries away. The sheriff never did get grandpa into jail because of his moonshine making.

Wade woke then. The dream had been vivid, almost real. He hadn't had a dream about his childhood for ages. That had been true about Grandpa outsmarting the law though. He really had been a bit of a stinker, Wade thought fondly, smiling at the memories. Slipping out of bed, he pulled the curtain aside and watched the snow fall for a while. It was getting pretty deep, he mused as he watched a young spike buck high-stepping through the snow on his way out of the lighted area. It stopped at the edge of the woods and looked back at Wade's cabin as though it knew he watched. Then it slipped into the snow-shrouded woods. Thoughtfully, Wade dropped the curtain and looked at the bedside clock on his way to the bathroom: 3:45 a.m. Taking a swallow of water before he left the bathroom, Wade sat on the edge of the bed and tried to decide if he wanted to try for more sleep or get dressed. Yawning, he slipped under the covers and settled in again. Maybe he could dream about Grams and Grandpa again. It was the only way he could see them now. It was better than nothing, he thought as he pulled the covers up to his chin. He turned the furnace down at night and it had cooled a bit, making the covers feel cozy. The next time Wade opened his eyes, it was full daylight. Very bright daylight. Glancing at the clock, he hastily threw the covers aside and hit the floor running. It was almost eight, and he was on duty at eight.

"No time for breakfast this morning," he grumbled as he hastily pulled on his uniform and trappings and grabbed his side arm and strapped it on. Running a comb through his hair, he grimaced at the stubble on his face but slapped his hat on and headed for the door. Locking up, he trudged through the knee-deep snow to the ranger station. Hopefully, Wilma would have coffee and doughnuts ready this morning. He didn't remember if it was her day to work or not. Guess he would find out when he got there.

The sun glare on the snow hurt his eyes. *Going to have to get sunglasses*, he thought as he stepped on the porch and stomped off the snow before opening the door. The smell of fresh brewed coffee registered as he closed the door and Wade looked up and murmured, "Thank you."

"Jess, how long have you known me?" Wade asked over his morning cup of coffee.

Eyeing him over his own cup of Wilma's coffee, Jess responded to the cryptic question with one of his own. "Why don't you just get to the point instead of starting the twenty-question game?"

Grinning wryly at his "get to the point" partner, Wade did just that. "Okay, have you ever known me to have a premonition? Like when the back of my neck prickles?"

Still waiting for Wade to get to the point, Jess said, "A time or two. If I remember you were right on the money with trouble being on the way. That been happening lately?" Jess asked as he took swallow of coffee and reached for another of Wilma's homemade doughnuts.

"Yeah, twice in the last twenty-four hours. I think Karnes has us under surveillance, waiting to strike at an opportune time. We have to smuggle your family out without him knowing, or he could go after them to use as leverage." Forgetting the doughnut, Jess agreed and got to his feet.

"Got any ideas?" he asked as he shrugged into his parka.

"Well," Wade said, "I think we could pass it around that we will be taking them to a scheduled doctor's visit and let him think they'll be back. With us along, he would probably want to wait for a better time hoping to find them alone."

"Good idea. Let's get things rolling. The luggage is in the trunk. He gets impatient, he might not wait for a better time, and I want them safe from that monster." Grabbing his hat, Jess headed for the door with Wade right behind him, trying to pull his parka on and grab his hat at the same time.

Heading for Jess and Sue's home after letting everyone know how lucky they were to get both Patty's and Peggy's appointments on the same day, they clued Sue in on the plan. And she took her largest purse with what essentials she could stuff into it and, after letting the two patients think they were on the way to see their respective doctors, loaded every one in the jeep and started the trip to Peggy's home. Patty objected to seeing her doctor twice in the same week but was quickly hushed by Sue and distracted by one of Wade's adventure stories.

After a good bit of slipping and sliding on the snowplowed roads, they finally turned onto a plowed highway and made much better time. Once they had some distance behind them, Jess told everyone what was happening.

"Sue can lease a car till the insurance comes through with the money for Peggy to buy one and Sue can borrow clothes from her sister. I believe Peg still has some clothes from the times that Patty spent time with her. That about takes care of it. I expect you all to keep a low profile for a while till we latch on to this guy. That means no unnecessary trips to town or anywhere else, everyone understand?" Everyone agreed, even Patty who didn't get it.

"We going to Aunt Peggy's? What happened to the visit to my doctor? I want my cast off. It itches awfully much," Patty complained trying to scratch under her arm cast.

"I have a big-screen TV and a lot of games to play on it," Peggy said conversationally.

That got Patty's attention, and she forgot about her itching cast. Before they arrived at Peg's home, she had the lowdown on every game that her Aunt Peggy owned.

Jess rolled his eyes at Sue, and she had a hard time trying not to giggle. She murmured, "We will probably appreciate the games before this is over. Why don't you stay with them and let me catch the bad guy? I have a feeling it will be the easier of the two choices."

Grinning, Jess returned with, "Not even on a bet!"

9

Aunt Peggy's house was an impressive, four-bedroom ranch type with two and a half bath; large living room and dining room; large kitchen, utility, and sun room with walk-in closets for each bedroom; and a wrap-around porch on two sides with two of the twenty acres landscaped and showing good care in spite of her absence for the last three weeks. She took care of the flower beds and the garden but left the rest to gardeners who kept it up and helped her with the rest occasionally. Not needed this time of year, of course, but they did keep the paths shoveled and the driveway plowed. The house sat in the center of the twenty acres with a curving driveway lined on the outer curve with willows, hence the name Willow Way on the arch at the end of the drive.

The well-shaded area behind the house boasted a fountain decorated with sea horses surrounded by a koi pond, and that was in turn surrounded by a large circle flagstone patio with raised flower beds around the edge. That was ringed in by various flowering shrubs. An eight-foot picnic table on a cement pad and a barbecue pit shared space under majestic old oak trees. Several various types of bird, squirrel, and deer feeders were scattered about the area being kept full by the gardeners. Not their job of course, but they liked Peggy and, since her accident, did it as a favor.

Sue never failed to be impressed with her sister's home and vowed one day to have a similar one. They had to stay in the ranger cabin for now because of Jess's job, but someday… she thought wistfully.

Having unpacked and settled in, more or less, Sue set about getting lunch. It was almost 1:00 p.m., and she knew everyone was hungry. Grating carrots for slaw while the Shake 'n Bake pork steaks cooked, she checked the potatoes and listened to Wade and Jess discuss the upcoming hunt for Karnes. Figuring out how to set a trap for the wily killer wasn't easy. In spite of his outward appearances, he was highly intelligent.

"I don't care how smart he is. We'll catch the bas…mfff." Wade stopped talking when Sue's hand landed over his mouth. She frowned and, nodding toward the just-arrived Patty, reminded them both, "Little pitchers have big ears."

"So do little kids," Patty remarked with an impish grin as she grabbed a peeled carrot and made for the living room to start another game, leaving them with open mouths.

Grinning and a bit red, Wade apologized. "Sorry, I tend to get a bit carried away sometimes when it comes to Karnes.

I don't believe Karnes knows about Sue's sister or where she lives. You all should be safe here. Keeping a low profile should keep it that way until it's safe to come back home. I'll tell everyone who lives nearby that might say something to keep it zipped. You going to make any more bread anytime soon?" Wade asked hopefully while helping himself to a carrot.

"Wade!" Sue scolded. "If you guys keep snitching the salad ingredients, I'll never get it done."

"It's just a carrot, and it's slaw, not salad," Jess said as he helped himself to one also and had to run when Sue grabbed the cutting board and started for him, scowling. Grinning, Wade made his exit also before Sue remembered that he was guilty of the same thing.

Coming back into the kitchen, Sue looked around for the second perpetrator and smiled at the empty kitchen. "Smart man," she murmured as she put the cutting board back on the table and set about finishing the meal.

Two hours later, with the meal consumed by appreciative appetites, the dishes in the dishwasher, and Peggy and Patty taking a nap, Wade and Jess were getting serious about the upcoming battle with Karnes. Trying to outthink him was one of the problems as he was not a rational man.

"We'll stay the night and leave first thing in the morning," Wade said as he settled into the recliner and stretched out. In spite of Peggy never having married, it was a man-sized one and very comfortable. Agreeing, Jess sat on the couch next to Sue and put his arm around her and gave her a hug before settling back. It would be a while before he'd see Sue and Patty again after tomorrow morning, Jess reflected glumly. He was going to miss them like crazy.

"Why don't you set some kind of trap for him?" Sue asked as she settled against Jess and relaxed. "Bait it with something you know he wants."

"He wants me, and I have to spring the trap, not be the bait," Wade muttered. "I want to be the person that gets his hands on him first. He's mine! If there's anything left, you can have it," he added grimly.

The next morning, as the sun topped the trees, Jess and Wade pulled into a gas station to gas the jeep and get something to eat. They had left at 4:00 a.m. and were reluctant to wake anyone for a meal at that time of morning—or night, depending on how you looked at it. Wade stated that it was morning, and Jess declared that it was still night. The bantering lasted most of the way to the point where they stopped for gas. With gas tank full and both of them chewing on sandwiches and sipping coffee, they resumed their trip with Karnes entering into the conversation, and they went to work on the plan of capture. A trap was a good idea, but what to bait it with?

The sun disappeared behind a rolling dark-gray bank of clouds, and Wade hoped fervently that they would make it home before the snow started again.

Taking it up to the speed limit, he held it as long as he could and finally admitted defeat when it started to snow and quickly turned into a whiteout with the wind hitting 30 mph. Creeping along, they peered through the snow trying to spot a motel. Finally spotting a lit vacancy sign through the whirling snow, Wade eased the jeep off the highway and stopped by the office.

"Can't travel in this," Wade muttered. "Better call and let them know we're holing up till it stops…They'll worry if we don't."

Agreeing, Jess started to climb out, and Wade told him to wait till he got the room. It wouldn't take both of them to do that. Wade climbed back into the jeep after securing a one-bed cabin, the only one left. They were lucky to get it as the storm had a lot of folks looking for shelter to wait it out. He had watched the *no* come on in front of the vacancy sign as he made his way back to the jeep and thanked the Good Lord for the one that they had found still available. Wade pulled alongside the row of cabins and stopped in front of number 7.

"Soon as we get our stuff inside, we can get a bite to eat before it gets too deep. Looks like some kind of quick-stop store just the other side of the motel."

"Okay," Jess agreed. "I'll make the calls while you get the stuff inside. Let me know when you finish."

"Will do," Wade muttered. Jess was going to load everything back into the jeep by himself when they left, he decided. Fair's fair.

Giving Jess the motel key, Wade opened the rear door of the jeep and got busy. Afterward, they headed for the convenience store.

Slogging back to the motel a half hour later, they had supplies for several meals. If this got a lot worse, the shelves could be empty the next time they went for food. Some of the equipment that Wade carried with him included a single-burner hot plate and instant coffee. Not his favorite kind but better than looking for a restaurant in knee-deep snow.

Bet Jess wishes that he had brought along his new snowshoes about now, Wade thought as he opened the cabin door and kicked off snow. Right behind him, Jess cleared his boots and leaned on the door to close it.

"Getting bad out there, he muttered. "Should have brought along my snowshoes. Would be a good time to try them out," he added.

"Sure would," Wade agreed with a grin. "The storm hit Peggy's place yet?" Wade asked as he set the groceries on the table in the small kitchenette.

"Just getting started while I was talking to Sue. I told her not to take any chances with it. Looks like a bad one. Peg's worried about the wildlife she leaves food out for. She didn't see this coming and hasn't restocked the feeders yet."

"They'll be okay till the storm passes," Wade assured him. "They don't eat in a storm anyway. Tell Sue that so she won't do anything foolish like going out in it to fill the feeders. She runs into a whiteout and she could lose her way. Better call back and tell her that. She don't like to see Peggy worry, figures she's been through enough."

"I'll do that, make me feel better if she promises to wait out the storm," Jess agreed, reaching for the phone again.

Wade fished out the instant coffee and plugged in the hot plate. Putting water in a small saucepan, he sorted out the groceries and set about putting a meal of sorts on the small coffee table while Jess made his call. Done with his call to Sue, Jess put the rest of the groceries away while Wade finished putting the meal on the coffee table. Wade turned on the small television hoping to get an update on the weather, and they sat down to a cup of hot coffee and food while the storm raged out side.

Makes a man feel positively snug, Wade thought. Good company, a snug shelter, and good coffee. *More or less*, he thought, looking at the half full cup.

"You heard anything more on Karnes's whereabouts?" Jess asked casually as he sipped his coffee.

"Nope," Wade replied as he checked the small fridge for snacks. "Been getting ready for bad weather and haven't had time to check in with the captain. I figure he'd let me know if he had anything come in anyway."

"I called the captain a while ago and let him know that were snowed in and where. Figured he might want to get hold of us if something came up," Jess said.

"Thanks, that'll save me a call."

Closing the door, Wade checked the cabinet over the sink and grabbed several snack bags of mixed pretzels and chips while wondering why Jess put them away when they were soon to be eaten. Probably done it automatically while thinking about something else, he concluded. "I've done that myself." Pitching them on the table, he returned to the sink and shut the cabinet door. Fishing in his suitcase, he pulled out a worn deck of cards and tossed them on the table with the rest. Closing the suitcase, he resumed his place at the table and, opening one of the snack bags to go with the rest of the skimpy meal, motioned for Jess to help himself.

After eating, Wade dealt the cards and, remembering Jess's last call, asked, "Sue promised to stay inside?"

"Yeah," Jess returned, going a bit red as he picked up his card hand. "Chewed me out royally for thinking she was stupid enough to have to be told not to go out in a blizzard. Said she was going to oversalt my gravy for the next month for that."

Grinning, Wade put down the deck and picked up his cards. "Sorry about that. I suggested you do that. You can tell her it's my idea."

"I'll do that," Jess agreed. "Might get me off the hook." Then muttered, "I hate oversalted gravy. Ruins it. That's hitting below the belt, literally!"

Several hours later, Wade and Jess hit the sack, with Jess using the couch. A bit short, he thought, but with Sue gone, it was better than a lonely cabin and a trip to it in this weather. "If we have to stay here tomorrow night, I get the bed!" he promised himself.

Ranger Wade

Persistent banging on the door woke Wade the next morning. Checking his watch as he reached for his pants, he groaned. Almost 9:00 a.m., he'd overslept. Jerking up his pants and fastening the front, he grabbed the shirt off the chair where he had pitched it last night and, running his hand through his hair, made for the front door, slapping Jess's shoulder as he passed the couch.

Pulling open the door, he noted at least another foot of snow and that it had stopped, at least for the moment. The second thing he noted was his captain glaring at him and panting like he had been running. Wading through deep snow did the same thing, Wade thought as he stood to one side and motioned his captain inside. Neither one had spoken yet, but Wade figured that whatever had brought the captain to his door in this, it had to be important. Jess had reported in yesterday after they stopped, letting them know where they were, but he didn't expect his captain to come looking for him. Looking outside at the roads, he noted that they had been plowed. *Slept through that*, he thought. *Must have been more tired than I thought.*

The captain had stomped off most of the snow from his boots on Wade's steps while waiting for him to answer the door, not easy considering the snow-laden steps. Shrugging out of his parka, he handed it to Wade and made for the kitchen, hoping for coffee. Looking in disgust at the cold remains of the nearly empty impromptu coffee pot, he stepped aside as Wade got busy making more.

"Why are you both still in bed? You sick or something?" the captain grunted as he pulled out a chair.

"Or something," Wade countered as he joined the captain at the table beside Jess, who was still yawning.

"What's up, Captain? You didn't wade through all that snow to ask about our health?"

"You're right, I didn't. Tried to call you, but the lines were down. Ranger Walters took out a snowmobile and went cruising this morning after the snow stopped just after daybreak. About a mile northwest of the station, he found the remains of a butchered elk yearling. Both haunches and the hide are gone. Wolves haven't found it yet, hasn't been there long. Jerry said it was still steaming."

Wade was fully awake now, and he felt in his bones that he knew who had killed the elk for food. Only one man would need to this time of year. Everyone else was gone.

"Karnes!" he stated flatly.

"Probably, but we don't know for sure. We have to act on the assumption that it was him though. He's too dangerous not to," the captain replied as he looked at the steaming saucepan.

Taking a hint, Wade rose, and fishing three Styrofoam cups from the bag, he measured coffee into them, filled them with the now-hot water, and brought two to the table and went back for his own along with cream and sugar packets. Impatiently, he returned to the sink and grabbed several plastic spoons from the bag. He tossed the spoons on the table and sat down again, reaching for the creamer packets the same time Jess did. Noting the grim look on Wade's face, Jess pulled his hand back and waited.

"What kind of tracks did he leave behind?" Wade asked as he added creamer to his coffee and stirred it. Glancing at the captain, he noted that he was still rather tired-looking. The snow was rather deep, but he should have recovered his breath by now.

"Snowmobile tracks and some kind of trailer," the captain replied, running his fingers through his hair tiredly.

"Captain, is there something you're not telling us?" Jess asked, deciding not to beat around the bush.

Sighing, the captain set his coffee cup down and leaned back in his chair. "Yeah, I guess there is," he muttered. "My last physical turned up a heart murmur. The doctor says I have a calcified heart valve and that it's time I retire if I want to keep on keeping on. The only other answer is open-heart surgery to replace the valve, and I don't plan on going that route. Soon as we collar Karnes, I plan on retiring. I am recommending Wade for my replacement if he wants it…do you, Wade?"

The question left Wade with his mouth hanging open. He had just been hit with a double whammy and couldn't seem to get his mouth in working order.

Swallowing with an audible gulp, Wade cleared his throat and managed to ask, "You want me to be captain of the ranger station?"

"Only if you want the job," the captain said with a grin. He didn't catch Wade by surprise very often, and it was rather satisfying. "You have enough experience to do a good job, and I would feel better about leaving if I knew you were taking over. What do you say?" Reaching for his coffee again, he took a swallow and made a face at the lukewarm stuff. Jess checked the hot water in the saucepan and, adding instant coffee to it, refilled the captain's cup.

Wade thought about being the captain, and it felt strange. He was content being what he was. It let him do outside work and enjoy nature.

"I don't want to sit behind a desk. I need to be in the field most of the time," he replied.

"If you're the captain, you can do what you want to," the captain came back. "What about it?"

"In that case, I'll take the job. First things first though, let's get serious about a plan to put Karnes back behind bars. I'd rather have a rogue grizzly loose out there than him…and the quicker we collar him, the better!"

Jess watched the exchange between his captain and his best friend and partner and was quite content to have Wade as his captain. He had no itch to be captain himself and cheered on Wade agreeing to take on the job.

Lifting his cup of coffee, he made a toast. "Here's to putting that creep back behind bars, and"—he looked at Wade—"to the new captain-to-be."

The other two lifted their coffee cups in a silent toast and drank.

10

Several mornings later, while shaving, Wade came close to cutting his own throat when someone knocked thunderously on his front door. Peering closely to make sure he hadn't, he laid down the razor and, grabbing the towel, wiped off the shaving lotion as he made his way to the front door. The knocking started again as he grabbed the handle and jerked open the door, prepared to give someone grief for scaring him like that.

The sight of Jess's agitated face cooled his anger, and he opened the door and motioned his partner inside.

"Can't, haven't time. I need to borrow your snowmobile sled. Mine is broken."

"Yeah, it's in the shed in back, what's up?"

"Jerry was on patrol this morning and found Shade about three miles north of here. He's been shot. Jerry called me on his two-way and stayed with him, and I came for the sled. I need it to bring him out of the woods so I can take him to the vet's. Can't get a vehicle to his location," Jess explained as they went around back with Wade pulling his jacket on without a shirt.

Kicking the snow from in front of the shed door, Wade forced it open and disappeared inside. He reappeared shortly, dragging the sled, and helped Jess hook it to his snowmobile. Watching Jess out of sight, he muttered grimly, "Something else I owe you for, Karnes." Closing the shed door, he made his way back inside and dressed for the trail. "Sure hope Shade makes it," he muttered grimly. "It would tear out Patty's little heart to lose him."

Climbing on his snowmobile after servicing it, Wade headed for the place that Jess said Shade had been found. His snowmobile was fast and powerful, and he made short work of the distance to where Jess and Jerry was just loading Shade on the sled. Seeing Wade, Shade lifted his tail in a weak wag. Swallowing the lump in his throat, Wade gave Shade a caress and muttered, "You'll be okay, boy, just hang in there, okay?"

"I got the bleeding stopped, but he's in pretty bad shape," Jerry told Wade. "He's lost a lot of blood. Looks like a hunting rifle of some kind. The bullet went through him, so we don't have a bullet to tell us what kind. Has to be Karnes that did that."

"Yes, and from now on, Jerry, you don't go out on patrol alone. That could have been you instead of Shade."

"Okay, Sarge. See you at the station later, Jess," Jerry said as Jess finished securing Shade to the sled and mounted.

"We'll follow you back, Jess. Soon as we load him into the jeep and you take off with him, I'll call the vet and tell him what happened. He'll have his surgery set up and waiting when you get there."

"Thanks, Wade," Jess came back as he hit the tree line and disappeared in the snow-shrouded woods.

Jess was looking apprehensive and angry at the same time, Wade noted as he and Jerry joined him in the vet's waiting room. His ranger hat had been twisted into an unrecognizable wad.

As they settled into chairs on either side of him, Wade murmured, "Hope you got another one of those. You kind of need them this time of year."

Giving Wade a blank look, Jess waited for an explanation.

"Your hat, or what's left of it. You planning on wearing that again?" he asked with a wry grin.

Looking at the remains of his hat, Jess threw it across the room and, leaning back in his chair groaned, "What the hell am I going to do if Shade don't make it? It will tear Patty's heart out. The poor kid's been through enough, she don't need to lose her best friend on top of it."

"If it helps," Wade replied, "I think Karnes has just made his first mistake. We now have a lead on his intentions."

Looking interested for the first time, Jess growled, "Explain."

"What would be the first thing you would do if you wanted to break into a house that had a big dog living in it?" Wade asked.

"I would get rid of the dog," Jess replied. Then his gaze sharpening, he growled, "You think he has set me up as a target?"

"Shade don't live with me. If he was going to break into my cabin, why shoot a dog that lived in someone else's cabin?"

"You think he's getting ready to snatch Patty or Sue? Maybe he isn't aware that they aren't here anymore," Jess murmured thoughtfully.

"We can set the trap at my cabin but will need some bait. We have to make him think that Sue and Patty are still here. We'll need to put some of her stuff in the yard and—"

The vet coming though the surgery door swung Jess around, and Wade sprang out of his chair and stood, waiting for the vet's verdict, with a fine sheen of sweat on his brow and hope in his eyes.

"Jess, Shade's going to be fine. He lost a lot of blood and the bullet broke a couple of ribs, but he'll be okay. I'd like to keep him for a couple of days to monitor his recovery, but you can come after him day after tomorrow. I'll give you some pills to help build up his blood supply again when you do. In the meantime, you might as well go home. He's unconscious and will remain so for the rest of the day. Give him time to start healing without too much moving around."

"Thanks, Doc, I owe you big time!" Jess replied, wringing the vet's hand. "I'll be back tomorrow soon as I get off duty to check up on him. Thanks again," he said, grinning happily. Heading for the door, he didn't see Wade and the vet grin at each other and Wade pick up what was left of Jess's hat as he followed him out.

The roads were plowed and passable now. Wade put his seat belt on and looked at Jess until, with a sigh, he did the same. Grinning, Wade pulled away from the vet's and headed back to the ranger station.

Relief made Jess talkative. He finally asked whatever happened to the fish dynamiter with the sick wife.

Grinning, Wade told him about Arnold's getting help with his wife, with a bit of help by Wade as he knew people and pulled a few strings. He grinned as he recounted the sorrowful tale he told the social service lady. She had a husband that was a bit self-centered but had long been accustomed to his ways. When Wade laid the story on her, it didn't take long to start the ball rolling. Arnie had the help he needed, and his selfless care for his wife had the social services lady walking through her front door with tears in her eyes; and when her husband stuck his face in hers and yelled at her because his supper was a half hour late, she decked him. When he looked up at her from the floor and yelled, "Are you crazy?" she had laughed all the way to the bedroom, locked herself in, and let him get his own supper. Grinning, Wade added, "If nothing else, I think it might have taught him a bit of respect where she's concerned.

"I also found out that Willow passed away just last week. It hurt Arnold terribly to lose her, but he was very glad that she wasn't hurting anymore."

"Sad story," Jess murmured. "Too bad they couldn't do surgery or something."

"The doctor that gave the first diagnosis thought more of his connections to his insurance company than his patients," Wade muttered. "The doctor that tended her last said that if she had seen him instead, he would have had time to do something for her. When he did see her, it was already too late."

Shaking his head that any doctor's Hippocratic oath didn't include putting patients before money, Jess climbed out of the jeep; and stomping snow off his boots, he pushed the cabin door open and flinched at the cold empty feeling. "I'll have some heat in here in a minute. Want some coffee?" Jess asked as he turned up the thermostat and headed for the kitchen. The ranger station and cabins all had furnaces but also contained woodstoves in case of a power outage, which happened frequently with the kind of weather northern Montana came up with.

Wade liked woodstoves. When he came in from bad weather, he couldn't snug up to a furnace. Thinking of woodstoves brought back memories of his grandmother. The scrappy woman was full-blooded Cherokee Indian. His grandfather had found her on the reservation while delivering a load of cattle, and they fell in love at first sight. He was twenty-seven and she only sixteen, but arrangements were made with her father, and they were married soon after her seventeenth birthday. Neither had ever regretted it.

Wade found a note in her Bible about a month after he lost her. It simply stated,

> I have no regrets with the life God gave me. I've been in a lot of other places but didn't like any of them near as much as home. I've watched the butterflies and wished they could stay year-round. I've watched and listened to the geese fly north and south and longed to join them—where they went didn't matter.
>
> I've longed for the green of spring after a long, hard winter, seemingly for a lifetime, and fairly danced when it was here. I felt like I had put money in the bank simply by planting something. I've listened to the wind, the rain on the roof, and the birds and gave thanks for them knowing they will be here long after I am not.
>
> When I was hurting, I'd plant or build something or do something that I've been putting off and feel better. When I was young, I danced for joy in the wilderness just because I felt good, with only God and nature to watch.
>
> I have loved and lost but will love again one day. I get the good stuff, ice cream, nuts and the like and enjoy all my minutes with loved ones but can relax

only at home. My life has been full but will get fuller one day.

When I want to build something, I don't wonder if I can. I simply tackle it. That's really the only way to find out if I can. I am in love with nature, peace, quiet, and the wonders that God gave us all. Unnecessary racket, crowds, etc., destroy that.

I will hopefully see you all again one day. Until then, know that I love you all…

Little Flower McKenna

"Sure, I got time for a cup," Wade responded, swallowing a lump in his throat as he came back to the present. "Then I need to find the captain and get the latest on Karnes."

Jess was pouring the coffee when someone knocked on the cabin door. Pausing, Jess put the pot down and headed for the door.

"Hi, Captain, come in," Jess said, stepping aside.

"I came to find out how Shade's doing," the captain said as he pulled off his gloves and shoved them in his pocket. Unzipping his parka, he hung it over the back of a chair and sat down. "Got any more coffee? It's Wilma's day off, and I can't make coffee fit to drink."

With a grin, Jess got another cup from the cabinet and, setting it in front of the captain, filled it and finished filling his own.

Taking a swallow of the hot brew, the captain sighed and set the cup down. "I needed that," he muttered. Looking at

Wade, he stated without preamble. "Karnes slaughtered a herd of elk. There were eight of them yarded up about six miles northwest of here, and he killed the entire herd. Must have used a silencer, or they would have scattered before he could get them all. He's laughing at us or wanting to make us so angry that we'll make mistakes, probably both." Hitting the table with his fist in disgust at the senseless waste, the captain grabbed his rattling coffee cup and took another swallow. Setting the cup down again, he added, "I sent the meat to the mission. Least it will do someone some good."

"Captain, Jess and I have been adding up things, and we think he's after a hostage to trade for me instead of Wade," Jess said as he slid into his chair and picked up his cup. "We believe he thinks Patty and Sue are still here and he'll go after one of them. That would be a good reason to get Shade out of the way. Jess will put some of Patty's stuff in the yard—her sled and skis. We will be setting a trap with the right bait and hope he takes it. We can rig up some kind of well-advertised get-together for the rangers that doesn't include family and leave the television and lights on. We can see Jess's cabin from the ranger station, and after all the vehicle's leave, we wait there with the lights out and see what happens. Might need to make it a two-day event. How does that sound? Think it will work?"

"Might," the captain replied thoughtfully, taking another swallow of coffee. "If it does, we have to make sure we latch on to him. Won't get another chance. Miss, and he'll disappear."

Getting to his feet, the captain paused while pulling on his parka. "By the way, when Shade is fit to travel, I'll have him delivered to Peggy's, and he can join the rest of the casualties." Grinning, the captain took his leave.

"Just what Sue needs—another patient," Jess said wryly as he said good-bye to Wade a bit later. "Have to let them know about Shades getting shot so they will know what to expect. I'll do that just before he arrives. Maybe I'll have good news about another problem by then. Need to tell the vet to let me know when he can send him to Peg's so I can warn them," he muttered as he watch Wade's long strides take him swiftly toward his own cabin.

"Hi Wilma, who's the munchkin?" Wade asked as he grabbed a sweet roll on his way to his desk with his freshly filled cup of coffee. He very seldom passed up the chance to drink coffee if Wilma made it. The woman had a magic touch when it came to cooking. Pausing in front of the window as he passed it, he watched Jess walking toward the station and, doing an about-face, grabbed another sweet roll. Jess really didn't have quitting sense when it came to Wilma's rolls, and Wade had gone back for his second one of the morning many a time to find them all gone and with Jess looking very satisfied. Ranger Jerry Walters met Jess by the door, and they came in together. Glancing at Jess as he hung his parka, Jerry made for the rolls and took his share to Wade's desk for safekeeping before he removed his parka. Hiding a grin, Wade sorted through the mail and other paperwork on his desk then grabbed a bite of his roll before heading for the captain's office for orders.

"She's my grandniece, Kitty Blessons, my brother-in-law's grandchild. Her parents are going on a weeklong cruise for their tenth anniversary, and I promised to babysit for the duration."

"I'm not a baby!" Kitty declared emphatically, reaching for one of the rolls and just beating Jess to the last one. Triumphantly, she took a huge bite while looking Jess in the eye. With a wry grin, Jess conceded defeat and returned to his coffee for consolation.

"I know that, sugar, it's just what everyone calls taking care of a child of any age." Wilma agreed. "Would you like some milk to go with that?" she asked.

"Nope," Kitty said around the last part of her roll. "All done."

"Okay." Wilma sighed. "Go wash the sticky off, and I'll see if I can find you something to do."

"Can I play in the snow?" Kitty asked hopefully.

"Wilma, can I talk to you for a minute?" Wade asked before she could answer.

"Sure," she replied. "We'll talk when I get back," she answered Kitty and followed Wade into his office and closed the door.

Waving her to a chair, Wade explained the proposed trap they were planning to set for Karnes. Trouble with the plan was there were no tracks made by a child or a woman around Jess's place since the snowfall happened after his family left. "You would be doing us all a big favor if you took Kitty to Jess's and let her play with the sled, maybe make a snowman. Leave a lot of your and her tracks to make Karnes believe Jess's family still lived with him.

"We will be sure to have a lot of movement by the rangers in the area to keep Karnes from seeing who leaves the tracks. Will you do that?"

"Sure, no problem. When do we start?"

"Thanks, Wilma, you'll have to wait until we make sure Karnes isn't in the immediate vicinity, then you two can start making tracks." He grinned at the pun.

"Okay," Wilma said a bit breathlessly. Wow, she had been working at the ranger station for almost two years now, but Wade's full grin still made her heart race. *Some woman will grab him someday, so fast he won't have time to duck. Hope I see it happen. Bet he fights it, but it's bound to happen.* Shaking her head and wishing she was thirty years younger, she went to find something for Kitty to do until Wade gave the all clear and they could go outside. Kitty would probably want to have a snowball fight too. "Been a while since I had one of those," she muttered. "Better wear a scarf to keep it from getting down my neck." Shivering a bit at the thought, she went in search of the protecting scarf just in case.

"Ranger convention, families, welcome on second day. Mandatory attendance on first day, all rangers. November 1 and 2. Be there! By order of Chief Ranger Warren McDermott," Wilma read out loud.

"Think this will work?" Wilma asked as she handed the paper to the captain. Reading it, Captain Jessup nodded and passed it to Wade.

"We still have to add where the convention is to be held, but I think it will be good enough to fool Karnes. What do you think?" he asked as he watched Wade read it.

"Good work, Wilma," Wade said as he handed it back. Naming a large VFW hall in the town nearest to them for the convention, he added, "Get hold of the administrator and make it happen, Wilma, and run off at least fifty copies of the announcement. I want to be sure that Karnes sees it. And while you are at it, you better get hold of Chief Ranger Warren McDermott and clue him in. If he sees one of the bills, he might start making waves at the wrong time and blow our cover." Turning to the captain, he inquired, "Sure Karnes isn't in the immediate vicinity?"

"I've had rangers crisscrossing the area since you requested it. If he's out there, he's in a hole. I think it's safe to start carrying out your plan."

Turning to Wilma, Wade gave her his best grin, effectively freezing her in place, and gave her the thumbs-up, "You're good to go. Start making bait tracks, Wilma."

With a salute, Wilma unfroze and muttered, "Will do, Sarge." And with only a slight stagger, she went to find Kitty to put the plan into action.

11

"Jess, will you get away from the window? The man has eyes like a cat. If he sees movement in here without the lights on, he'll know it's a trap."

"Sorry, Wade," Jess whispered. "But how're we going to know when he gets here if we can't look out of the window?"

"Stand back from it and stand still. You have on dark clothes and only movement will give us away. Have some more coffee, it will keep you alert."

The moonlight on the snow and the outside yard light gave them good vision. The snowman made by Kitty and Wilma, sporting the hat that Jess had mangled in the vet's waiting room, stood out in stark relief against the dark woods. The lights in the cabin were hooked up to timers, and the one in the living room just went out a few seconds after the bedroom light came on. Jess had done a good job setting the time on them.

Wade had had the timers for quite a while and never used them. One of his sisters gave them to him for a birthday present, and he'd put them back and forgotten them until yesterday. Thank goodness he hadn't given them away as he intended to. Pouring coffee by what little moonlight reflected in the window was tricky business, and Wade was concentrating on the attempt when Jess hissed, startling him into spilling some on his wrist. With a silent curse, Wade set the pot and cup down and wiped the hot liquid off his wrist as he moved quickly to Jess's side. "Look at the right corner of the cabin, I saw movement there. Keep your eyes on it," Jess whispered, easing back to put on his parka. Easing up to Wade, Jess handed him his parka, and they watched as Wade pulled it on and checked his side arm.

"We have to close in fast. It won't take him long to find out the cabin's empty," Jess muttered as they waited for Karnes to enter the cabin.

"He isn't going to go into the cabin," Wade said as he relaxed and grinned at Jess.

"How do you know he won't?" Jess growled, taking another quick look.

"Because it's a black bear. He went into the garbage can you keep by the corner of the cabin. Probably a last meal before holing up for the winter." Wade grinned at his discomforted partner.

"Well," Jess muttered, "it could have been him. Better not to take chances."

"You're right about that," Wade conceded, giving his partner some slack. "Karnes might not go in either," Wade added. "If it were me, I'd try to catch one of them outside and away from anyone else. Even if he doesn't see anything suspicious, he might sense a trap. He's half-animal when it comes to survival."

Thinking about either Sue or Patty in Karnes's hands had Jess growling, "That's one animal I wouldn't mind seeing in a cage."

Suddenly, Wade tensed. "Jess, heads up. The bear just took off like it was being chased."

Silently, Wade and Jess watched the cabin, and what they could see of the surrounding area intently. After a half hour, they relaxed, and Jess made another pot of coffee.

"You think the bear got a whiff of us?" Jess inquired as he poured coffee for them both.

"I doubt it. Wind's been in the same direction since this morning. He was that scared of us he wouldn't have come in the first place. Had to be something new that he didn't like. Might be a cougar, but he didn't act like it—too scared. Man's about the only thing that scares a bear like that. Our smell is all over the place. He's used to it. I have a bad feeling that our chance to capture Karnes has come and gone, at least for tonight. We'll wait till the rest get back and mingle with them so Karnes won't know we were in here. Might get another chance at it."

Yawning, Jess nodded, then said okay when he realized that Wade couldn't see him.

"You want more coffee?" Jess asked an hour later as he shook the pot to see how much was left.

"No, I'm coffeed out. You can have it," Wade responded as he scratched an itchy armpit. "Man, I could use a hot shower, the captain and company should be getting back pretty soon. What time is it anyway?" he inquired, knowing that Jess had a glow-in-the-dark dial on his watch.

Pulling back his sleeve, Jess muttered, "It's half past one. No wonder I'm pooped. Hey, I think someone's coming now." Watching together, they waited until the jeeps came to a stop and everyone piled out then made their exit and joined them. The captain didn't say anything until they were inside the ranger station with the lights turned on then sailed his hat at the elk rack and snorted in disgust when it fell to the floor. Picking it up, he glared at Wade, who was doing his best not to grin.

"Anything happen?" he asked as he carefully placed his hat on the rack. Pulling out his chair, the captain sat down and sighed with relief. "Must be getting old. Staying up late didn't used to bother me much. Now I feel like I've been dragged through a knothole backward."

"Nothing unusual," Wade responded as he brought another chair for the update talk. "Bear got into the garbage can then took off like he'd been shot at. Might have been a cougar or a grizzly, but I intend to take the snowmobile out in the morning and look for tracks." Turning to a yawning Jess, he asked, "You coming?"

"Sure, just throw a stick of dynamite in my bedroom. It should wake me up. When do you want to leave out?' he asked with another yawn.

"Dawn," Wade replied and grinned when Jess glared at him. It was too easy to get a raise out of Jess. "About nine will do. The tracks won't go anywhere, and you need your beauty sleep." Laughing, Wade hurled the empty Styrofoam cup into the trash bin and, putting the chair back, picked up his parka. "Hit the hay Jess," he relented. "Even nine will come early enough. Night, Captain," he said as he opened the door and leaving Jess at his cabin. Soon he opened his own cabin door and welcomed the warmth. It had been a long day, he decided. Better luck tomorrow night. Flipping the light switch, Wade's jaw hit the floor. It looked like a tornado had found its way inside and had trouble getting back out again. No wonder that bear had took off. Karnes had hit Wade's cabin while they were watching Jess's. Probably laughing his rear end off while trashing it.

Cursing silently, Wade viciously hurled his hat at the antler rack and didn't even notice when it bounced off the wall above it and hit the floor. "That's another one I owe you for, Karnes!" he snarled out loud.

Grimly, he rolled up his sleeves and went to work, trying to straighten out the mess. Two hours later with the cabin back into some semblance of order, Wade showered and crawled into bed, hoping he could sleep. No such luck. It was almost 4:00 a.m., and he was still too angry to go to sleep. Shifting up on his elbow, he set the alarm for 7:00 a.m. He didn't need it most of the time, but he had a feeling he would in the morning. Lying back down, he tried to calm his mind and relax.

Nothing worked. Dawn the next morning found him staring at the faint light coming in the east window. Giving up, Wade crawled out of the bed and headed for a wake-up shower. Six o'clock found him eating a breakfast of cold pizza and coffee, still in his bathrobe. Putting the dirty dishes in the sink for later attention, he wandered into the bedroom and dragged out the uniform that he intended to wear for the day. Digging into the drawer for underwear, he momentarily relaxed with a smile as the act reminded him of Jerry's pink polka-dot boxers. It had turned out better than he had hoped. The trip turned Jerry's reluctance to something else before he dropped the captain's niece off at her house. They had even made plans to go to the movies in the town nearest to the ranger station on the following weekend.

Coming back to the present, Wade gave a jaw-cracking yawn and decided to get another cup of coffee before dressing. It wasn't even time to even get out of bed yet; he had plenty of time.

Filling his coffee mug to the brim, Wade turned off the coffee pot and carefully carried it back to the bedroom, and after taking a swallow, he noticed his unmade bed. Shaking his head, for he usually made it soon as he got out of it, he started to set the coffee down on the nightstand when the alarm went off and the coffee went flying all over his unmade bed. "Another one I owe you for, Karnes!" he growled in frustration. Then with a wry grin, he muttered. "Could have been worse. I might have already made the bed."

Looking at his now mostly empty cup, he added wryly, "I'm awake now anyway…and talking to myself again… Karnes's fault," he growled. Taking the cup back to the kitchen, Wade stripped the bed, thankful that the covers had contained the coffee and the mattress was dry. Getting sheets from the closet, he made up the bed and added an extra quilt in place of his usual blankets.

"Have to let Wilma know that I need these washed. She'll probably wonder where all the stains came from, but" he added, "she will be too polite to ask." He thought fondly of the lady.

Bunching the stained bedding, he crammed it into a large trash bag and left it by the front door. Glancing at the wall clock, he yelped and dived into his uniform and boots and, with a hasty comb through his hair, grabbed his hat and parka and bolted out the door. His shed door did not want to open; it was packed with crusted snow. Wade had to kick it loose before he succeeded in gaining entry. Pushing his snowmobile out into the light and checking the gas and oil, he started the engine and let it warm while he secured the shed. Glancing at his watch, he groaned. He was always on

Jess for being late. Something told him that Jess wouldn't pass up the opportunity to get even this morning.

Mounting the growling snowmobile, Wade hit the gas and, sending snow into the air behind him, streaked toward the ranger station where he was to meet Jess. Pulling up in front, Wade killed the engine and looked around. Jess's snowmobile wasn't in sight yet. Maybe he had lucked out. The warmth hit him as he walked in the front door and looked around for Jess. The first thing he noticed that Jess wasn't there, the second was the smell of fresh coffee and rolls. Wade's mouth watered as he realized that he hadn't had supper last night and didn't have time for breakfast this morning. What he had found when he walked into his cabin had pushed the thought of eating right out of his mind.

Throwing his hat at the rack, he grabbed his parka and noted as he removed it that the hat had settled on the rack in the usual manner and that he had earned another glare from his captain. Grinning, Wade poured himself a cup of coffee and grabbed a couple of fresh rolls and made for his desk to do justice to them. He was well into his second roll and beginning to feel human again when Jess walked into the door, looking sheepish.

"Sorry about being late. I forgot to set the alarm," he explained as he shrugged out of his parka and made for the rolls. Pulling up a chair, Jess joined Wade at his desk, and Wilma smiled as she set a cup of coffee in front of Jess.

"Thanks, Wilma, you're a lifesaver," Jess muttered around a mouthful of sweet roll.

Watching the exchange between Wilma and his partner, Wade thought of his own stained bedding and wished that he had also forgotten to set his alarm.

Finishing up their quick breakfast, such as it was, Wade and Jess were soon on their way.

"Captain said that he met a friend of yours last week when he took April back to her dormitory," Jess said as he headed for his snowmobile. "He was doing yard work and general maintenance for the college. Name of Sully Kunes. Kunes said to say howdy for him," Jess yelled over the roar of the his engine.

"Kunes isn't what you would call a friend," Wade responded. "The last time I seen him, I was testifying at his trial for hunting elk out of season. He had four of them on his trailer covered with pine trees. Said he was getting Christmas trees for his family. If Shade hadn't given him away, he might have gotten away with it."

Rounding the ranger station in an ever-widening circle, Wade and Jess found tracks of a large man with a long stride. Following them led them to snowmobile tracks that ended at the nearest usable road. Truck tires continued on from there.

"He loaded the snowmobile into a truck by himself. Strong man," Jess commented.

"Karnes is quite strong," Wade agreed. "I had trouble subduing him when I arrested him. I heard later that he was doing weight training for competition in prison. He won't be a piece of cake to whip now for sure. I just hope I can get the drop on him first and won't have to do a hand-to-hand with him…I might not win this time," he added grimly. "Nothing else we can do here," he added. "Let's split and check out the area while we're in the field. You know what to look for. You have your radio?"

"Yep, always carry it with me," Jess returned as he patted his pocket. "Meet you anywhere or back at the station?" Jess asked as he tightened his hat.

The Russian fur hats weren't regulation but were a heck of a lot warmer than the ones that were. Pulling his own down a bit tighter, Wade raised his voice. "Back at the station. Don't be late. I don't want to have to come looking for you," he teased, reminding Jess of his hour-late arrival for their meeting this morning.

Grinning good-naturedly, Jess gave him the thumbs-up, and they both hit the gas and took off in different directions.

Working in ever-widening circle, Wade and Jess found several elk herds yarded but undisturbed. They were accustomed to the sound of the snowmobiles, and besides shifting uneasily and keeping an eye on them, the elk refused to break out of the packed area. Finally, the sun was low in the sky; and getting low on gas, they both headed back to the ranger station, arriving only minutes apart. After parking in front, they went inside to make their report.

"I can see why Sully isn't any friend of yours," Jess had remarked loudly just as they both killed the engines when they met in front of the ranger station. And Jess asked in a lower voice when he seen the pained look on Wade's face, "Just out of curiosity, Wade, is Sully, Kunes's real first name? If so, why would any mother hang a name like that on an innocent newborn?"

"It's short for Sullivan. I investigated him after I arrested him. Was going to give him a break if it was a first offense, but it's apparently an ongoing lifestyle for him," Wade answered as he preceded Jess through the station door.

"Hey, Captain, anything new on that Karnes character? Anyone seen him?" Jess hollered as he closed the door and followed Wade toward the captain's office as they didn't see him in the front room.

Coming from his office, Captain Jessup frowned at Jess but didn't bother answering. Motioning them into his office, he closed the door and, waving them to chairs, returned to his chair behind the desk.

"Jess, I overheard you mentioned that Kunes was not a friend of Wade's. Care to clarify that?" the captain asked.

"You heard me from inside?" Jess asked, looking surprised.

"You weren't exactly whispering," the captain answered dryly.

"I can answer that, Captain," Wade said. "Three years ago, or thereabouts, I arrested Kunes for hunting elk out of season." Telling about his experience with Kunes took about ten minutes including answering questions the captain asked. When finished, the captain asked Wade to make a brief report on paper.

"I have an idea that Kunes will have another reason for hating rangers, I'll have to write the headmaster at April's college and let him know what kind of person Kunes is and will include your report. His record of arrests speaks for itself. He's been convicted of a felony and isn't allowed to work for any school. When he loses his job, he might come after you like Karnes, and they might even join forces."

"Captain, I haven't told anyone yet, but when I entered my cabin last night, it had been trashed. Whoever did it was very thorough. It took me almost two hours to put things back to right and clean up. I'll have to replace some of it, but it wasn't as bad as it looked at first. But it was bad enough to make me want to get hold of whoever did it in the worst way. I didn't tell anyone because only us and whoever did it knows what happened. I'm hoping someone will let something slip not knowing that it isn't general knowledge."

"Christ, Wade, why didn't you let me know? I would have helped clean up," Jess asked, upset that Wade had excluded him from something so important.

"No need of both of us losing sleep, Jess. I need another lock on my back door also, Captain. Whoever did it broke mine. I need to restock on groceries also."

"I'll see to it, and, Jess, the vet called a while ago. He's shipping Shade to Peg's in the morning. You told Sue what happened to him yet?"

"Nope," Jess groaned. "Didn't want to do that till I had to. They'll see for themselves that he's all right soon as he gets there. Sue will probably chew my rear out good for not letting her know that he was hurt. It'll be a year before I get decent gravy again, you wait and see," he moaned.

"Better call and get it over with," Wade said sympathetically while hiding a grin. Jess did love his gravy. "Patty will be glad to have Shade with her again, wound and all." Wade tried to reassure him then changed the subject. "Anything else came to light on Karnes, Captain?" Wade asked as he rose from his chair and turned to wait for his partner and missed a strange look on the captain's face.

"I'll let you know if anyone sees him in the vicinity," the captain returned evasively.

"Thanks, Captain. Let's go Jess. You got a phone call to make, and I need to catch up on some sleep."

Watching them walk out the door, the captain sighed, thinking that he might be in for some butt kicking also sooner or later. "Face it when it gets here," he muttered, and letting himself out, he locked the door. His cabin was located behind the ranger station—the closest one—and he would be handing it over to Wade soon. "Maybe Wilma could do some fall, er, winter house cleaning for me," he mused as he opened his door after kicking the doorjamb just to be sure the snow was off his boots. The path was beaten down by now, but it did tend to become a habit.

Feeling a cold draft, he turned to make sure the front door was closed. Finding it so, he noticed how cold the house was. The furnace was running, and he began checking the windows. The back bedroom window was up and letting in the frigid evening air.

"I did not open that window!" Jessup muttered, slamming the window shut. After checking every room, he relaxed and began to laugh. "Idiot took my television. Probably didn't know how to operate a computer." Chuckling, he set about fixing supper and went to bed. Tomorrow was another day after all. Don't sweat the little things and you can handle the big things a lot better when they come along. His dad's wisdom had helped him more than a few times over his lifetime. Smiling, he relaxed and slept the sleep of the just.

The next morning after telling Wade about the break-in, Captain Jessup settled into his chair with his first cup of coffee of the day. Looking longingly at the doughnuts on the kitchenette table, he sighed and took a sip. Not as young as he used to be, he had to start watching his weight. He had noticed a bit of a spare tire beginning to appear and decided to squelch it before it got too noticeable.

"Your cabin was broken into yesterday? Captain, why didn't you say something?"

"I didn't know it until I got home yesterday evening, Jess. By then it was too late to catch him. He opened a window, he didn't break in. Besides," he said with a grin, "he only took my television. I couldn't find anything else missing." His grin getting bigger, the captain added, "It quit working over a month ago. I was wondering what to do with it when I got around to getting a new one. Don't have to worry about it now. The man actually did me a favor." Smiling contentedly, Jessup leaned back in his chair and took a sip of his coffee.

"Some people have all the luck!" Wade muttered, remembering what he found when his cabin had been broken into. Catching a knowing grin on his captain's face, he grabbed his parka and hat and stalked out in disgust.

Heading for the captain's cabin, Wade found footprints, but the snow was too deep to leave a clear impression. Digging down to the actual print led to better results. The pattern on the bottom of the boots that had left the prints was like a hundred others in this area, except for one difference. The left one was missing some of the pattern where the man had stepped on something sharp and tore a chunk out of the pattern of the heel. "Find something, Sarge?" Jess inquired as he waded through the drifted snow.

"Come and look at this print. It has a distinctive mark that should help us identify the owner."

"Yep," Jess agreed. "Now all we have to do is go around and look at the bottom of everyone's feet." Chuckling, Jess yelped when a snowball hit him in the side of the head. "What's that for!" he asked indignantly.

"Not in the mood for sarcasm," Wade growled and headed back to the station to let the captain know about the damaged boot, leaving a bewildered Jess in his wake. Wade was very seldom in a bad mood. Getting under way in the deep snow after fishing the snow out of his collar, Jess waded out to the packed area and made for the station where Wade was just disappearing inside. "This bears checking into," he muttered, and quickened his pace.

"Wade, can I impose on you to give me a ride to town?" Wilma asked as Wade walked in the door. "I've been getting a bit dizzy on occasion, and my doctor wants me to come in for an exam. Said it could be a lot of things and can't make a diagnosis long distance. I have an appointment for two o'clock this afternoon."

"No problem," Wade answered, looking concerned. "I need to pick up a few things anyway. When do you want to leave?"

"Right after lunch, if that's okay," she replied with a sigh of relief. She was not good at driving on snow-packed roads; they scared her to death.

"I'll pick you up at your house," Wade assured her. He knew about her aversion to driving this time of year. She walked the distance from her small rented cabin when she worked, and one of the rangers picked her up in bad weather. The captain said it was the least he could do as she wouldn't allow them to pay for the doughnuts and sweet rolls that she brought to the station. Said it was therapy to cook, and if they didn't help her out with the results, her therapy would make her too heavy to get in the station door. He wanted to provide transportation all the time, but she had said she needed the exercise but would accept on bad days.

"How long you going to stay in town?" Wade asked as he checked his mail. All mail was delivered to the ranger station and was picked up there.

"That depends on what the doctor finds," she said as she got ready to work.

"I'll work till noon and go home and have lunch and get ready. I'd better pack a bag in case he wants me to stay a while," she answered as she settled in her chair and got busy. It would be a short workday, and she had to get busy if she expected to make any progress on the pile of mail on her desk. Thinking longingly of a good hot cup of coffee to help her with the task, she sighed and pushed it out of her mind. Doctor visits were a pain.

Jess walked in the door in time to hear the most of the conversation. He liked Wilma a lot. The station just wouldn't be the same without her, not to mention her sweet rolls and doughnuts, he reflected gloomily. Jess walked up behind Wilma and, bending, gave her a quick hug and made a hasty exit, leaving her surprised but pleased at the gesture of affection.

Wade watched his partner's quick exit with an uncharitable thought. *He'll miss the doughnuts and rolls the most if she don't return*, he summed it up then gave himself a mental kick. *Jess isn't like that, what am I thinking?* Shaking his head, Wade made his exit behind Jess to start his timber-cruising rounds.

"Been by myself too long," he muttered. "Getting grouchy." Tightening his hat, he started the snowmobile and let it idle as he waited for Jess to come back with his. Shortly they were off and headed for the yarded elk first to check on possible poacher activities.

"Wonder what Karnes will come up with next. The captain nearly blew a gasket when he found out about the yarded elk being killed," Jess bellowed over the engine noise.

"Hard telling," Wade yelled back "Need to watch everything as much as possible. He could strike anywhere.

Hope he don't hit the yards anymore. Captain couldn't take another slaughter like that. It could cause a heart attack. We need more rangers up here until he's caught, we're spread too thin."

"I agree," Jess yelled. "Maybe we should ask the captain to request more men. It couldn't hurt to try."

"I'll talk to him when we get back," Wade hollered and pulled ahead of Jess to stop the talking. At this rate, he would soon be hoarse.

Grinning, Jess knew what Wade did and didn't mind. It was rather hard to hold a conversation anyway. Normally, they would split up to cover more ground, but the rule now was to stick together for safety reasons. Karnes would love to catch one of them alone.

The next yard was a large one. It contained a dozen elk of various sizes and age, from the bulls to this year's calves. It was undisturbed. Circling wide, they continued to the next one. They did find another butchered yearling that the wolves had been at, but there was no other evidence of any more activity by poachers. Checking out the kill, Wade said, "Someone is living on game. Just takes the haunches. He has to be holed up in the park somewhere. It could be Karnes," he muttered.

"Think it's the same guy that broke into the captain's cabin?" Jess asked.

"Nope, he wouldn't have electricity to run the TV he stole. Besides, Karnes knows how to operate a computer, and he would have taken that instead of the TV. This guy don't act like I think Karnes would, and the tracks were different. Karnes wants revenge in the worse way. Not enough action in stealing a small television for him."

Looking at the cloud-filled sky, Wade decided to head back. It was starting to look and feel a lot like snow, and he didn't want to get caught a long way from the station when it started. "Time to head in, Jess. This one is coming in fast. Book it! I'll keep up with you."

"See you there, Sarge," Jess yelled as he swung back toward the station and gunned it, leaving a rooster tail of snow in the air behind him. Grinning, Wade tightened his hat and followed. Jess did love to open these things up.

They pulled into the station before the snow started, but after reporting to the captain, they walked outside into a blizzard.

"Wow, sure glad we didn't get caught a long way from home in this!" Jess said as they loped to their respective cabins. "See you in the morning, Sarge," Jess called as he veered off toward his.

"Maybe," Wade muttered as he pulled his door open. Looking back, he couldn't see the station or Jess's cabin. "Might just have a day off tomorrow."

Closing the door, Wade pulled off his parka and hung it on the row of large nails and sailed his hat at the antler rack. Grinning smugly as it caught, he headed for the bathroom for a wash, then to the kitchen.

13

"I hate this inactivity. When is Karnes going to make his next move?" Jess muttered as he stared gloomily out of the station window at the added foot of snow that had accumulated over the last week.

"He probably won't for a while, Jess. New snow leaves too many tracks and is difficult to get around in. I am beginning to wonder. Things just don't add up to Karnes. If it is him, he's doing a lot of beating around the bush. He's the kind to go for the jugular," Wade answered, closing the file cabinet after inserting his latest report on the poaching. "Captain, have you put in the request for more men? I would like to catch this guy soon as possible before he hits another yard full of elk."

"I believe we can handle the problem, Wade," The captain said, giving his roll a lot of unwarranted attention. "If things get worse, we can always holler for help. In the meantime, I have full confidence in your ability to deal with it."

Clearing his throat, the captain grabbed his half-empty coffee cup and headed for the coffee pot for a warm-up.

Why do I have the feeling that there is more going on here than meets the eye? Wade thought, watching Jessup fill his cup. Putting his own in the sink, he motioned to Jess and, pulling on his parka, grabbed his hat and left the station. Following close behind, Jess closed to door and, mindful of the way that sound carried in the clear frigid air, waited for some distance before asking, "What's going on Wade, what's the captain up to?"

"I don't know Jess, but I intend to find out. We might as well have a look around. Whoever is butchering the elk might just leave a clue next time that we can use."

"When's Wilma coming back?" Jess asked hopefully. "I sure miss her rolls and coffee. It will take a bit of recovery time after drinking the captain's coffee, and these store-bought rolls just don't taste the same as hers. Think we could hire someone to do the stuff that Wilma was doing till she does? What did the doctor find out about her getting dizzy anyway?"

Finally getting a word in edgewise, Wade responded regretfully, "She won't be back, least not for quite a while. Doctor put her on special medicine, and she has to have close monitoring. She plans on staying with her brother and his wife until spring. She'll decide then if she will come back."

"Who's going to handle the paperwork till then, Sarge? And the idea of drinking the captain's coffee till spring is an excuse for early retirement!"

"Captain said they were sending someone to handle the paperwork, another woman. She will take over Wilma's cabin. Last name of Kenyon. Didn't hear the first name. Her mother and Wilma were best friends and also became sisters-in-law, then Wilma moved into the cabin here, but they kept in touch. Wilma recommended her for the job. I believe Wilma said that they still send letters to each other once in a while," Wade said as he climbed on his snowmobile and tightened his hat.

Jess followed his lead and they were soon deep in the forest following snow-laden trails, the sound of the motor muffled by the deep snow. The next yarded elk they checked on hadn't been so lucky.

"Think we should let the captain know?" Jess asked, gazing mournfully at the eleven slaughtered elk.

"We have no choice in the matter, Jess, maybe we can get some help now. This is going to hit the captain hard. I get my hands on this guy, he'll look like your hat did before the vet told you that Shade would recover."

Thinking about that for a moment, Jess grinned and asked, "Can I watch?"

"If it's Karnes, you might have to help capture him. Won't be much time for watching. Come on, we better let the captain know about this. He'll want to salvage the meat for the mission soon as possible." With a last long look at the carnage, Wade turned slowly and climbed on his machine and left the scene followed closely by his partner. Neither felt like talking.

Wade was right about the captain's response to the news about the elk slaughter. He blistered the air in two languages and paced in the small confines of his office for a good ten minutes before calming down enough to start making plans for the disposition of the carcasses. His phoning finished, the captain glared around for a few seconds as though he didn't know what to do next. Then slumping in his chair, he ran his hand through his hair and growled, "I'm getting too old for this. Wade, I want that bastard bad. I don't care what you do to accomplish it, just get him!"

Getting carte blanch from the captain told Wade how upset he really was. "I'll do my best, sir. Anything new on Karnes?" he asked before he left.

"Er, no, nothing has come in lately. If anything does, I'll let you know," Jessup muttered as he got busy with the paperwork on his desk.

Eyeing him for a second, Wade turned and left. Something was going on. What the heck was the captain up to anyway?

Jessup gave a sigh of relief when his sergeant finally left. He would have to let him know what he had been withholding from him soon. But damn, he wanted Wade after the elk killer in the worst way—no holds barred. If anyone could trap him, Wade could. Sighing, he looked at his half-full coffee cup and rose to pitch it in the sink. *Never could make coffee worth drinking. Be glad when the new secretary gets here. Hope she can make good coffee. Be expecting too much to hope for rolls and doughnuts too*, he thought mournfully. "Might as well request the help Wade's asking for. Really do need it, even without the elk killing. He's getting suspicious anyway, it might sidetrack that for a while. Geez! Listen to me talking to myself like an old grandma. Wade better hurry up and get this guy. He's driving me around the bend!" Looking at his watch, Jessup locked up the station and headed back to his cabin. Maybe supper and a good-night's sleep would help a bit.

The volunteers to haul out the slaughtered elk arrived about the time that Wade was thinking about supper, but he put it on hold and geared up again and led them to the yard that held the slaughtered elk. Without further ado, the men got busy field dressing the elk to lighten the load, and were soon loading the sleds that two of them brought behind small snowcats. Finished, Wade circled the area checking for tracks while waiting for the volunteers to finish loading and found another young cow in the woods where she had collapsed after trying desperately to escape the slaughter with a bullet in her lungs. Calling the others, they soon added her to the load and left. The elk were to be delivered to a slaughterhouse that handled wild game. With a minimum charge for processing, they processed, froze, and stored it until the mission needed it. This amount of meat would feed a lot of families for a long time. *The silver lining to the black cloud I guess*, Wade thought tiredly. But for the love of God, if the two butchered yearlings were also the victims of this madman, he was responsible for killing twenty-two elk in less than a month. Pulling off his parka and hat, he cleaned up a bit and went to the kitchen and stood looking in the fridge, not seeing a thing he was interested in eating. But he needed to keep his strength up. Pouring a glass of milk, he made a sandwich of last night's fried potatoes and added a couple of slices of bacon from this morning's breakfast and, with a little mustard, called it supper. It didn't taste too bad, he thought. Something he used to put together when he was a teenager. *It still works though*, he thought as he ate. Putting the plate and glass in the sink, he turned out the light and called it a day. *Maybe tomorrow would be better, couldn't be much worse*, he thought.

The next morning, seven rangers and ten volunteers arrived to lighten the workload so they could concentrate on getting the poacher. The latest slaughter convinced the powers that be to send help. Making full use of the additional help, Wade immediately set in motion a series of roadblock and checkpoints leading in and out of the park. Even the trails were watched by volunteers. All traffic was stopped, and the vehicle searched for game and weapons. Everyone had a picture of Karnes and instructions to arrest any one with game or rifles in their vehicles. No tickets, no exceptions. Any rifles found were to be taken to ballistics in Great Falls for a match to the bullets removed from the slaughtered elk. If Karnes was spotted, instructions were to report him and wait until help arrived to apprehend.

Things are looking up a bit, Wade thought as he checked in with the captain to give him an update on the progress made. "Captain, are you all right?" Wade asked as he noted Jessup's pale countenance.

"Not really, Sergeant, I think I better head for town and see my doctor. I've had a lot of pressure on my chest since I got here this morning, and it isn't going away. I need you to drive me in."

"Will do, Captain, I'll get the jeep and be back in a second." Wade made short work of his mission and was in front of the ranger station waiting for his captain in short order. Spotting Jess coming toward the station, Wade hollered, "Jess, I'm taking the captain to town. You're in charge till we get back. Hold down the fort, will you?"

"Will do, Sarge. Special occasion?" Jess asked as he headed for the jeep.

"Tell you when I get back." Noting that the captain was in and had his seat belt buckled, Wade slammed the door and took off a bit faster than he usually drove on snow-covered roads, leaving Jess staring at the back end of the jeep, wondering. "What now?"

14

Watching Wade pull up in front of the station several hours later, Jess noticed that he was alone. Soon as Wade came through the front door, Jess asked impatiently, "Where's the captain, Sarge?"

"In the hospital. He was having a heart attack. It was a mild one but could have caused permanent damage if we had waited any longer. He should have asked for help soon as the pressure started and didn't go away. With his heart murmur, you would think he would know better. He is retired as of now, Jess, I am now the acting captain until it's made official," Wade said and waited for Jess's response.

He relaxed when Jess responded with, "So now what's our next move, Captain? You made any more plans, or do we wait to see if the roadblocks catch anything?"

"We wait."

The next morning while sorting through the paperwork to see if anything needed immediate attention, Wade started at the knock on his door. Looking up, he motioned at the person he could see through the glass while taking another drink of his first cup of coffee of the day—and nearly swallowed the whole cup as a tall female ranger walked through the door. Setting his cup down, Wade rose and offered his hand.

"You here to take care of the paperwork?"

At her nod, he motioned to a chair; and when she sat, he resumed his seat and waited for her to start.

"My name is Loraine T. Kenyon. I am twenty-nine years old, five foot seven, blond hair and green eyes, and one hundred and twenty eight pounds. My middle initial is a need-to-know thing only. I am here as punishment for smacking my superior for assuming too much about our relationship. It was that or a suspension. When the paperwork catches up with me, you can confirm that. In the meantime, I am ready to go to work. Where do I start?"

"Thanks for being up-front. The desk to your right as you leave my office will be yours. You can start by grabbing this lot and doing something with it. The situation here is a bit unusual. When you catch up, we have to talk about that. In the meantime, I want you to know that I do not make moves on the help, no matter how beautiful they are."

Eyeing him for a second, Corporal Kenyon nodded and, gathering the papers off Wade's desk, made her exit.

Wow, why didn't someone warn me? he thought, pouring another cup of coffee, his hand a bit unsteady. The new secretary was the exact opposite of Wilma—tall, willowy, blond, green eyes and a french braid extending halfway down her back. In or out of uniform, she would knock your socks off.

Wilma, are you doing the matchmaking thing? he silently asked the absent lady. The ringing of his phone put an end to speculation. After hanging up the phone, he opened the door and motioned the new secretary into his office. Waiting for her to enter, he closed the door and, finding his seat right after she did, began to talk.

"Corporal, may I call you Lorraine?" Getting her nod, he continued. "Lorraine, I need to explain the situation here in this area. It's been on going for several weeks now and is rapidly getting worse." Starting from the first incident, Wade told her all pertinent facts of the elk killing, break-ins, and their subsequent actions up to the present time.

"Reports are coming in from the roadblocks, and I need you to keep track of them and handle things here for a while. My partner and I will be doing a lot of fieldwork until the elk killer is caught but will check in with you once in a while. Can you handle it?"

"Yes, sir, anything else?"

"Yeah, forget the sir thing, call me Wade or Captain, will you?"

"Yes si—captain," she replied. Smiling, Wade handed her a sheaf of papers and, dismissing her, answered the phone again.

Sitting the papers down on her desk, Corporal Kenyon fumed silently, *What am I getting into? Out of the frying pan and into the fire—that had to be at least a thousand-watt smile. I need another superior that looks like a movie star like I need another hole in my head. What did I ever do to deserve this?* She looked at the ceiling briefly.

Barging into the station an hour later, Jess skidded to a stop and checked out the new secretary. Ignoring him for a few seconds, Lorraine finally asked, "Can I help you?"

"Yes, ma'am. I'm corporal Jess Beal. I was Sergeant McKenna's partner until he was made captain. I guess I need another one now. Will you be my partner?" he asked with an infectious grin.

In spite of the obvious flirting, Lorraine found this ranger likeable and returned his grin. "I'm corporal Loraine Kenyon, and I can't—too busy. You should ask the captain about getting another partner, Corporal Beal."

"Okay…um…can I ask you a question?" Jess asked. At her nod, he asked hopefully, "Can you make good coffee? The last secretary did, but Captain Jessup tried to poison us with his after she left, and it might be what eventually did him in."

"I make good coffee," she assured him and grinned at his obvious relief. "I also make rolls and doughnuts just like my Aunt Wilma does. As a matter of fact Aunt Wilma taught me to cook." She laughed out loud at his euphoric expression at that bit of information. *Maybe this place won't be so bad after all*, she thought as she watched him head for the captain's office. *If that hunk in the office don't spoil it*, she added. Why didn't her Aunt Wilma warn her about the new captain? Was she matchmaking? If she was, it won't do her any good.

I need a man, like, when I get too old to be a ranger maybe. Then I'll have the time perhaps for all the demands they make.

Diving into Wade's office, Jess blurted, "Sarge, er, Captain, guess what? She can make good coffee, and she also makes rolls and doughnuts!"

"I guess we lucked out with the head office's choice of a replacement, didn't we?" Wade said, enjoying Jess's obvious happiness.

"We sure did, Captain. Do I get another partner? I want her." He grinned.

"You don't need another partner, Jess, I'm still your partner. I plan on doing a lot of fieldwork and I'll need my partner for that."

"Good," Jess said with relief. "I kind of like the one I have. Besides, Sue probably wouldn't like the idea of me partnering with Lorraine."

"Me too, and no, she probably wouldn't. Now get out of here. Don't you have an assignment yet? If not, I can give you one."

Checking his watch, Jess admitted to having one already and giving Wade a snappy salute, he made his exit, grinning at the new secretary on the way out.

Watching Jess till he left the building, Corporal Lorraine Kenyon summed it up. "I have a feeling this place does not have a problem with boredom."

Watching the door absentmindedly after Jess's exit, Wade thought of the trill of laughter he had heard from the front office a few minutes ago. There was something different about the new addition to his staff that made him aware of her as he had never been aware of a female in his life. He had seen a lot of beautiful women in his career—none had left a permanent impression like this one might.

Best keep my distance from this one. I don't need any distractions right now.

The call came in a week later just before lunch.

"Captain, we caught someone at the west roadblock. He had a .407 magnum rifle with him, and he was headed into the park. He's handcuffed and sitting in one of the park jeeps."

"What's his name?" Wade snapped.

"Well, he wouldn't say, but I dug his driver's license out of his pocket after we handcuffed him. It's Sullivan W. Kunes."

"He gets away, you're in trouble. I think he might be the one that's killing the elk. Stay put, I'm on my way." Breaking the connection, he called Jess and told him to be ready to go in five minutes. Slamming down the phone, Wade grabbed his gear and bolted for the door. Stopping in front of Loraine's desk, he gave her brief instructions what to do and who to contact in case of trouble. Anything else that she couldn't handle could wait. Getting her nod, he bolted out the door and climbed into the jeep. Pulling up in front of Jess's cabin, he honked the horn and gave it the gas soon as Jess was seated and still putting on his seat belt.

"Okay, give!" Jess growled, giving Wade a steady look.

Glancing over at his partner, he snapped, "I am not sure, but we may have caught the elk killer at one of the roadblocks." Giving Jess the details took several minutes. They were closing in on their destination as he finished. Pulling up at the road block, Wade showed his ID and drove through to the car that held the prisoner. Getting out and taking a deep breath, Wade prayed for this to be the right one.

Sully fit the profile of the killer, in every way. He should have connected him to the elk killings when the first yard was wiped out. It was, after all, too petty for Karnes. Being half-Indian made him more or less respect nature, and killing elk for revenge was not his style. He would simply go after the one he was angry at. When Jess joined him, they walked to the jeep containing Sully without a word, each thinking about all the elk that had paid the price for this petty thief's revenge.

Motioning to the ranger in charge, he waited till the jeep door was opened and stepped closer. He bent down and looked into the sullen eyes of the suspect. Glaring at Wade, Sully refused to speak, maintaining a sullen silence.

"Just couldn't let it go, could you, Sully? Couldn't take the punishment you earned like a man and start new, you had to hang on to your self-righteous anger, and now you're in the soup again. With the six I caught you with the first time and the two butchered yearlings, you are responsible for the deaths of twenty-eight of God's creatures that never harmed a soul."

Glaring, Sully still kept silent. Wade wanted, in the worse way, to haul Sully from the jeep and beat him to within an inch of his life, but that's something Sully would do. Looking at Sully with intense contempt for another few seconds, he had the satisfaction of watching red creep up Sully's neck.

"Let me see the bottom of your boots," Wade ground out with a glare that Sully decided not to challenge. Struggling sideways in the cuffs and seat belt wasn't easy, but Sully finally held up his right boot for Wade's inspection.

"Now the other one," Wade snapped as Sully lowered the right one and brought the left one up. His eyes fastened on the mutilated pattern on the sole, and Wade said, "Thanks, you can put it back down now."

Stepping back, Wade slammed the door and gave the order for the jeep's driver and two guards to take Sully to Columbia Falls and turn him over to law enforcement and get the man behind bars. Killing elk, since it happened on federal property, was a federal offense. It would be a long time before Sully Kunes killed another elk.

"Tell them that I'll be in soon as possible to file charges. And watch him, he's tricky." Nodding, the driver chose two of the rangers to accompany them as guards and left with the prisoner.

Heading back to the station, Wade let out a deep breath and murmured, "Sure glad that's over. Or at least it will be when he's convicted and behind bars again."

"He was pretty mad last time," Jess said, looking at Wade. "What's he going to be when he gets out next time?"

Looking at Jess for a second, Wade turned his attention back to the road and replied, "I'll have to cross that bridge when I get to it. If he's lucky, he will learn his lesson this time around. If not, I guess things will hit the fan again."

"Yeah," Jess muttered. "Next time, he might aim for you instead of the elk."

Wade had no reply to that. It was a very real possibility.

15

Letting his partner off in front of his cabin, Wade said as Jess started to exit the jeep, "Jess, I need to go into town to file charges tomorrow. You're in charge while I'm gone. I need to see Captain Jessup also. Catching the elk killer will make his day."

"Okay, Captain. How long you planning on being gone?" Jess replied as he got out of the jeep.

"Half day, maybe, two o'clock at the latest. I have some shopping to do, and I want to check on Wilma also. Anything comes in on Karnes, let me know soon as I get back."

With a snappy salute, Jess slammed the jeep door, getting a glare from Wade. And with a grin, he went into his cabin.

Watching the cabin door for a few seconds, Wade grinned also. Jess was hard on doors, but he was a fine partner. He did have a sense of humor, but he could get serious darn fast when the need arose. Whistling a catchy tune, he put the jeep in gear and pulled away from the cabin and headed home. It was late enough to call it a day—a very successful day, he added to himself with a good deal of satisfaction.

Wade left right after breakfast the next morning. First on his agenda was filing charges against Sully. He would recommend that he be held without bail as he was a real flight risk. Second was to visit his former captain in the hospital and give him the good news about the capture of the elk killer.

With charges filed and Sully secured, Wade headed for the hospital.

"You can't stay long. He just had surgery and needs his rest. You have five minutes," the stern-faced nurse told him.

"Yes, ma'am," Wade replied with one of his best smiles and headed for the captain's room before it hit him what the nurse had said. "Surgery? I didn't even know he was scheduled for one!"

The nurse appeared to be shell-shocked for a few seconds. Then with a mental shake, she watched Wade disappear into the captain's room and turned to resume her duties, wishing she were younger. He did tend to have that effect on older women.

Slipping into the captain's room, Wade's gaze centered on the figure on the bed. Seeing movement, he murmured, "Captain?"

Jessup turned his head enough to spot his sergeant and smiled. "Hi, Wade, it's been a while. How's things going?"

"Good news, Captain. I believe we caught the elk killer. It was Sully Kunes."

The captain's eyes widened, and he answered breathlessly, "That's the best news I've heard since I got here."

"I didn't know you were to have surgery, Captain. I would have been here if I had," Wade said, looking concerned.

"I wasn't originally," Jessup muttered. "One of the new nurses got my medicine mixed with another patient's, and I had a reaction. They thought my heart was quitting, and they did an emergency valve implant surgery. It was over before I knew it was going to happen. When another patient had a reaction taking my meds, they investigated. Stupid mistake, but it gave me a new lease on life, so I don't plan on suing anyone over it."

"Time to go, Captain. The patient needs his rest," the stern-faced nurse insisted, and Wade said good-bye and headed for the door.

The captain's voice stopped him. "Wade, look on top of the tallest file cabinet. There are some papers that you need to see."

"Okay, Captain, see you later." Wondering what that was about, Wade left the hospital and headed for the grocery store. Finished with his shopping, he checked on Wilma. And after a short visit, with the promise of another visit in the near future when he had a bit more time, he headed home.

A hot bath and a good cup of coffee seemed just the thing right about now. He would check out the papers that the captain mentioned later. Tomorrow was another day. He whistled his way most of the way home with a tune he couldn't seem to get out of his head, and he couldn't even remember the name of it.

Lying awake when he should be sleeping at one fifteen in the morning, Wade blamed his inability to sleep on an unanswered question. If Kunes was causing all the problems, where in thunder did Karnes disappear to? He couldn't give Jess and his family the all clear until he knew, although Karnes didn't have anything against Jess and family. Still, better not take chances with a mentally deranged killer. His actions would not be predictable now, at least not compared to his past habits.

Speaking of Jess's family, he hadn't heard from Jess yet on what Sue's reaction had been on learning about Shade being shot and on the way to her for postoperative care. *Been a good time to be a fly on the wall and listen in, bet she gave him what for. I'll ask him tomorrow.*

Yawning, Wade punched his pillow and tried to relax and think of something good. At 2:10 a.m., he got up and raided the fridge for milk and a sandwich. *Empty stomach can keep a man awake*, he thought. *But so can three cups of coffee just before bedtime.* He groaned.

The next morning, Wade awoke to his alarm with approximately two hours of sleep under his belt and, groaning, turned on his side and reached out an arm and hit the snooze. Ten minutes later, he did the same. Finally on the third try, the overworked alarm was successful, and he crawled out and got ready for duty.

"If I weren't the captain, I believe I'd play hooky today," he groaned. Finally, clean-shaven and dressed, he pulled his parka and hat on and headed for the station.

Opening the ranger station door, he looked up when the smell of fresh coffee and rolls hit his olfactory senses. Pulling his parka off and hanging it on the hook, he sailed his hat at the antler rack and took it for granted that it would catch—it did. Heading for the lifesaving coffee, Wade filled his cup and grabbed two rolls and, sitting at his desk, made short work of them. Feeling a lot better, he went back for a second cup and came face-to-face with his new secretary, also on her way for a refill.

"Good morning, Captain, I trust you slept well?" To tell the truth, she thought, he looked a bit like he had a hangover.

"Not really," he grumbled. "Too many things on my mind. Come into my office. I need to give you an update on what's been going on around here."

Waving her to a chair, he took another swallow of coffee. And sitting his cup down, he leaned back in the chair and for ten minutes, told her play by play about the warning about Karnes's escape and the arrest of Kunes and Wilma's progress with her health and the accidental medicine mix at the hospital that caused the captain's impromptu surgery.

"You have been very busy, I can see that costing you sleep, but with Kunes in jail and the captain doing well, why didn't you sleep last night?"

Grinning, Wade admitted to three cups of strong coffee before bedtime. "Kind of like a letdown, I suppose," he admitted. "I couldn't get the thought of what happened to Karnes out of my mind either. There's been absolutely no sign of him since he disappeared, it's like he vanished off the face of the earth. I know the man's half-Indian, but even an Indian would leave some trace, and Karnes hasn't left a single one. I can't bring Jess's family back until I know what happened to him.

"From what you've told me about his character, I wouldn't either," Lorraine agreed. "Would you like another cup of coffee, Captain?"

"No, thanks, Corporal, I'm coffeed out. Thanks anyway. I feel almost human now. A good cup of coffee was what I needed to wake up. The rolls didn't hurt anything either, thanks for bringing them. You seen Corporal Beal this morning?"

"Yes, he's checking the elk yards. He said that since Kunes was in jail, he didn't figure the pairing-up rule was still in effect. He isn't convinced that Kunes butchered the two yearlings that you found."

Frowning, Wade said grimly, "When he gets back, remind him that Karnes is still out there somewhere, and the partner rule stands. Tell him that I'll have his hide if he takes off alone like that again before I personally rescind it, will you?

I'll be in town catching up on things and should return by noon. When Jess comes in, tell him to stay put until I get back, I need to talk with him." He pulled on his parka and took his hat off the antler rack.

"Yes, Captain, anything else?"

"No. Hold the fort, will you? Thanks again for the rolls. We sure did miss them when Wilma left. One of the things I want to do is check on Wilma again and see how she's doing. We didn't have much time yesterday for catching up on things. If she wants to come back when she's able, you can take the field again. I gathered that being a secretary isn't your favorite field of work. She's one of the family around here. We miss her."

Smiling at the thought of Wilma and the way she had fit in here at the station from the first, Wade left, not seeing his new staff member's expression.

"Drat the man. Why does he have to be nice along with being so gorgeous? That's just not fair!" she wailed.

"Jess, I think you can call Sue for an update on Shade and the other invalids and let her know what's happened on this end. I'm more or less convinced that Karnes is headed in the other direction because he believes that we'll be watching for him around here. My guess is that he'll lie low until things die down and we relax, then he'll strike. He won't be gunning for dogs and trashing cabins either. If I'm not available, take ranger Walters on your next round. You hare off again by yourself and I'll put Corporal Kenyon in the field and you can take her place. Comprende, senyor?"

"Loud and clear, Captain," Jess muttered, his neck a couple of shades darker from the chewing out. He admitted to himself that he had it coming, but that didn't make it any easier to swallow. He had forgotten about Karnes in the excitement of getting the elk killer.

"By the way," Wade changed the subject. "Ballistics confirmed that the bullets taken from Kunes's rifle matched the ones taken from the slaughtered elk. With his boot prints matching the ones outside the captain's cabin, he is now out of the picture. But Karnes still has to be dealt with sooner or later. When you're in the field, keep your eyes peeled."

"Yes, sir!" Jess came back with a snappy salute.

"By the way, you missed the rolls that Lorraine brought this morning. They tasted just like Wilma's," Wade said and grinned when Jess groaned.

"Aw, Wade, that's hitting below the belt!" Jess's shoulders slumped, and he headed for the door totally dejected.

"But," Wade called before Jess closed the door, "she saved a couple for you." He laughed long and loud when Jess hurriedly popped back in and asked where they were.

Watching the byplay from her desk, Loraine groaned at the unfairness of it. "Drat the man!" He was undermining the heck out of her assessment of men in general. She had to rethink where the captain was concerned. He didn't fit her profile of captains at all! They usually thought they had a right to do what they wanted, with her as well. Her objections to that got her the present assignment.

The last captain she served under had agreed to reassign her rather than face her in court on sexual misconduct charges. He had been luckier than he knew; she had a black belt in self-defense and could have quite easily put him out of commission for a while instead of threatening him with legal action. She readily agreed as she was quite happy to be done with him. Any place would be better than where he was.

This captain showed no inclination for that sort of thing, thank the Good Lord. However, if her attraction to him kept growing and she didn't find out anything about him bad enough to slow it down, she would have to watch herself or be in trouble for trying to jump his bones. There was no indication that he found her attractive. He had been, she suspected, avoiding her when he could. But why did he do that if he was indifferent?

"Is it possible that he is fighting his attraction to me?" she asked herself, wondering how she was going to find out the answer to the million-dollar question.

Wait and see what develops, I guess Bet he hasn't had a problem like that before. Probably just the opposite. It should be interesting anyway. He probably left a string of broken hearts behind him and didn't even know it. If he is attracted to me, maybe its time for paybacks? she thought hopefully.

Wade, unaware of his new corporal's plans for him, chose to accompany Jess on rounds this afternoon. He needed to get away from civilization for a while and soak up the peace and quiet that only nature provided.

Jess emerged, wiping icing off his mouth as Wade pulled up in front of the station. And grinning at his happy expression, Wade told him to grab his machine and meet him at his cabin in ten minutes. Heading for his cabin, Wade made a call to get an update on Shade's progress and find out how Patty and Peggy were doing. Happy with the news of all the patients being in a fast recovery mode, he said his good-byes and hung up as Jess pulled up in front.

Climbing on his machine, he gave the sky an assessing look and decided to make it a quick round through the yards. "This one will have to be fast, Jess. We got a couple of hours before we start having more weather. You heard the weather report today yet?" he asked, waiting to start his motor.

"Not this morning," Jess replied. "But last night, the weather report did mention more snow on the way and maybe some wind also. Cause drifts in some places, I reckon. Not supposed to hit until late, but it don't look like it wants to wait that long," he added.

"Right you are, Jess. Stay close and circle the station in widening circles. You don't see any tracks in an hour, head in. I don't like the looks of that sky. Some people use storms for cover when poaching, though, and if you're right and Sully didn't kill the two that were butchered, we still have an elk killer to deal with." Settling his hat firmly, he snapped, "Let's do it, Jess."

As one, they hit the gas and sped into the snow-laden forest, Jess circling to the left and Wade to the right.

Meeting each time a circle was completed, they called a halt and headed in after the hour was up. And leading the way, Wade noticed that it was getting colder, and the wind was picking up. The icy wind reminded him of his granny again as they sped toward the ranger station under an ever-increasing threat of bad weather. On one of their many trips to the grocery store with so many mouths to fill, they were met on the way out of the store by wind and rapidly falling temperature. Hugging herself with one arm as she was using the other to push one of the filled grocery carts, she muttered, "Whew…where's a hot flash when you need one?"

Another customer, headed into the store, overheard the remark and simply hee-hawed. Wade got a good laugh out of it himself, part from his granny's remark and part from the reaction of the other man.

Coming back to the present, Wade parked in front of Jess's cabin and waited till Jess turned off his motor. "Jess, I'm going to tell Corporal Kenyon to button it up for the night. Anything she hasn't finished can wait till after the weather clears. If it's still blowing in the morning, stay home." Getting a nod from Jess, Wade started his motor again and headed for the station.

Corporal Kenyon had just finished up the paperwork and was thinking about Wade and wondered if he had a girlfriend tucked back somewhere that no one knew about. When he left the station, it was, for the most part, business.

She washed the coffee pot and got it ready for the morning and had just turned out the small kitchenette light when Wade came in and slammed the door against the rising wind. "Getting bad out there, Corporal. Better call it a day. I'll give you a lift back to your cabin if you like. This could turn into a whiteout. I just got another secretary, I don't want to lose her in a storm," he added with a grin. Looking outside, Loraine agreed with him and grabbed her parka and hat and was soon gliding over the snowpack behind Wade. Hanging on to Wade wasn't a hardship at all, she decided. In fact, it was rather nice. Grabbing on harder when Wade hit a bump, she thought, *Yeah, pretty nice*, and decided that she wouldn't mind if he hit another bump.

Pulling up in front of her cabin, Wade watched until she unlocked her door. Then waving, he took off. And hitting the woods trail, he opened it up and, when a mile from the station, gave an Indian war cry. A threshing in the shrubbery and quick flight from several birds that had been settling in for the storm let him know that the animals didn't share his exuberance.

"Sorry," he muttered in apology to the disturbed wildlife and, with a huge grin, headed back toward his cabin. Needless to say, he had very good dreams that night.

———ϕνϕ———

Waving in response to Wade's wave, Lorraine unlocked her door and, with a last glance at the retreating figure on the snowmobile, closed it and leaned against it. "It was only a ride home," she chided herself. "Don't make anything else out of it." Easier said than done, she decided two hours later after making sure the wood rack under the overhang in back was full and the ashes out of the woodstove. She filled several gallon jugs with water and figured she was ready in case of a power outage. She looked around for something else to do to stay occupied. Then glancing at her watch, she decided, hopefully, that supper, a hot soak in the tub, and a good-night's sleep would sort her out.

———ϕνϕ———

As predicted, the storm was still raging the next morning. Wade stood at the window looking at the whirling, windblown snow and contemplated going back to bed, but knew he wouldn't get any more sleep. With a huge yawn, he headed for the shower. *Be a good time to catch up on things around here*, he thought ten minutes later while turning off the shower and reaching for a towel. Fishing in his underwear drawer for clean briefs, he inevitably thought of Jerry and his polka-dot shorts.

"Wonder how he's getting along with the captain's niece now? Things were warming up real nice last I heard. Might have a wedding one of these days…better his than mine," he muttered as he pulled on his underwear.

But for the life of him, he couldn't keep the willowy figure of his new corporal from imprinting herself on his imagination. He would love to undo the french braid that hung down to the middle of her back and watch it fall down its full length. He bet she could sit on it. And her grabbing him when he hit that bump almost made him pull over, but he thought better of it and kept going. He grinned when he thought about his looking for another bump to hit like some randy teenager. *Good thing I didn't pull over. She would have smacked me in the chops like she did her last captain. Might have been worth it though.* He grinned again at the picture that brought to mind.

Checking the storm again as he passed the bedroom window on the way to get a uniform from the closet, he decided to wear Levis today. He had cleaning to do, didn't need a uniform for that.

"Wonder if Corporal Kenyon does laundry?" he thought aloud, looking at his depleted wardrobe. Shrugging, he pulled on Levis and added a long-sleeved shirt over his T-shirt. Pulling slippers on over his socks, Wade headed for the kitchen for a cup of coffee and breakfast.

An hour later, breakfast over and the dishes washed, he stood looking out the window trying to see the station. Giving up, he ran his hand through his hair and wished the storm would let up. Thinking about Captain Jessup in the hospital brought back the memory of his instructions concerning some papers on top of the tallest file cabinet.

"Should have checked them out yesterday when I was there, had other things on my mind I guess," he conceded, thinking about the ride home he had given his corporal with her arms wrapped around him. He would have liked to have turned around and hugged her back. He had worked up a pretty good head of steam just taking her to her cabin, and, soon as he dropped her off, had booked it for distance and released it. It had been a long time since he did that. "Felt pretty good," he decided, but didn't think he would do it again. *Too hard on the wildlife*, he thought with a grin.

He had started practicing a war whoop soon as he found out he was quarter Cherokee and had gotten pretty good at it. But like most teenagers, he had tended to carry it to extremes, and his dad had finally made him quit. Whistling, he rolled up his sleeves and went to work on his early spring house cleaning.

Corporal Kenyon was also doing her spring house cleaning. She had to do something or go nuts. She couldn't quit thinking what it felt like holding on to the hard muscled figure of her captain during the snowmobile ride yesterday.

She thought of what it would be like to have those powerful arms wrapped around her instead of the other way around and got goose bumps. She squelched a frustrated whimper.

Was she ready to have a man's ego imposed over hers? Oh yes, women did have egos. They just weren't as important as a man's in the natural scheme of things. Women also had pride, but not a lot of attention was paid to that fact either.

Those two problems were one of the main reasons that she wasn't already married, or at least engaged. The last man she got serious about assumed that she would give up her ranger career and stay home and entertain his guests when he decided to throw a party. His pride forbid that his wife should work. He told her what he expected as soon as they became engaged. He had filled his pipe with an expensive cut of tobacco, and when it was going well, he removed it from his mouth and quietly began laying down the marriage rules, finishing with the last rule: "I will wear the pants in my family, not negotiable on that point." Finished, he placed the pipe back in his mouth and waited for her agreement on the matter. She listened patiently until he was through explaining how it was going to be. Then without saying a word, she pulled of her engagement ring, handed it to him and left. She didn't even look back.

"Put that in your pipe and smoke it!" she muttered bitterly as she headed for home. She wanted a partner, not a blasted owner. Slavery was supposed to be illegal the last she heard. Apparently her former "intended" hadn't heard that little fact. He had showed up at her door several days later after waiting a reasonable length of time for her to "come to her senses" and take her ring back. She slammed the door in his face and finally had to request a transfer when he wouldn't take no for an answer. Her next position netted her a captain with the same leechlike tendencies, and when he cornered her between the corner and a file cabinet, she gave in to her frustration and smacked the stuffing out of him. He went into a rage at the thought of being struck by a subordinate, let alone a woman, and threatened her with dismissal and assault. Had he but known it, he lucked out that she still had that much control and he only sustained a beautiful black eye and a nosebleed. Being a black belt had taught her to control her temper as well as self-defense.

When she could get a word in edgewise, she had quietly threatened him right back with a sexual harassment lawsuit. Glaring at her in a frustrated rage while holding a handkerchief to his copiously bleeding nose, he had jumped at her suggestion that he transfer her to another station. She suspected that he didn't want it to get out that he had been decked by a woman.

She had wound up here and had liked it from the first day, never mind her new captain. He was okay also—more than okay, she admitted with a grin. If he was any more okay, she wouldn't be able to keep her hands off him. She just might be having a bit of that kind of trouble anyway, she decided.

Trying to get him out of her mind, she scrubbed the inside her cabinets to within an inch of their lives. Then washed every dish in them before replacing them in neat stacks and rows. Then she washed the curtains and bedding and remade the bed and was looking around for something else to do when the knock on her door brought her to a halt. Glancing out the window on the way to the door, she noted that the snow had almost stopped. Jerking open the door, she was surprised to see Wade standing with a large laundry basket and patiently waiting for her to invite him in, or at least ask him what he wanted.

"Captain, I wasn't expecting anyone, is something wrong?"

"No, nothing wrong, Corporal, except that I'm about out of clean clothes. Wilma made extra money by doing washing on the side, and I was wondering if you wanted to pick up where she left off?"

Grinning, Loraine asked, "Don't you know how to use a washing machine?"

"Yes, I do, but your cabin is the only one equipped with a washer and dryer. It was too expensive to install them in all the cabins. Captain Jessup only did it to keep us from running off to Columbia Falls to use the Laundromat. He put them in Wilma's when she promised to do all the washing for the ranger station."

Seeing the question in his eyes, she stepped aside and motioned him in. Shutting the door, she turned and caught him looking around at the sparkling clean cabin.

"Spring house cleaning, right?" he asked with a wide grin that nearly knocked her socks off.

Bracing her suddenly Jell-O like knees, she nodded. "Nothing else to do," she muttered breathlessly. Grabbing the basket out of Wade's hands, she headed for the utility room, adding, "I'll have this ready for you tomorrow morning."

"I appreciate it," he drawled and, taking his dismissal in good grace, headed for the door.

"Captain, thanks for the ride home yesterday," she said as his hand closed on the doorknob.

Turning to look at her as he made his exit, he smiled and said, "You're welcome, Corporal. See you in the morning."

"If you keep doing that, I may have to get braces for my knees," she muttered to the closed door. Fanning her too-warm face, she decided to start the wash and bring it with her when she reported for duty in the morning.

Wade paused on her step, enjoying the memory of the blush he seen as he closed the door. She wasn't as indifferent to him as she pretended to be, he decided happily.

Blast it! Where in thunder is Karnes? When he's corralled, I might just get serious about the idea of courting. Until that happens, I won't have the time to do it properly. Besides, he finds out that I care about her, he might try to take his hate out on her, then I would have to kill him instead of putting him back in prison. Something else I plan on taking out of your hide, Karnes! First, lady, I think about getting serious about, and you get in the way of that too!

Slamming into the station, Wade did a double take when Jess dropped his coffee cup on the kitchenette floor.

"Why the heck don't you just shoot me!" Jess growled as he looked at the mess on the floor.

"Sorry, Jess, I was thinking about Karnes again. Any more coffee in the pot?" he asked hopefully. He could use a good shot of something right about now.

"Yeah, I asked Wilma for a coffee recipe when I visited her a few days ago, and this is the first time I could try it out. Corporal Kenyon has been making it. She coming in today?" he asked hopefully, thinking about rolls or doughnuts coming with her.

"No, I told her wait till the morning. Today is half gone anyway."

"Oh well, I'll get you a cup soon as I clean this up. The phone is still working, that's good news. We lucked out this time. Storm like that usually takes out the electric and phone both. Hope Corporal Kenyon brings doughnuts in the morning. They sure go good with her coffee."

"Jess, is everything all right? You're doing a nervous chatter. That means something's up. Give!"

"Aw, Wade. I miss Sue and Patty something fierce," Jess groaned as he put the mop back in the small closet by the sink. "My cabin's awfully empty without 'em. When can I bring 'em home anyway?"

"It shouldn't be much longer, Jess, I miss them too."

The next day, having completed the monthly reports, Wade decided to check on his captain again. Leaving Jess in charge and heading for Columbia Falls Hospital, he tried to devise a plan to find out where Karnes had disappeared to. It wasn't possible for him to simply disappear. He had to have left some kind of trail. He might never show up here, and he couldn't keep Jess and his family separated forever. Reluctantly, Wade decided to tell Jess to bring them home, and if Karnes did show up, they would simply have to deal with it.

Pulling up in the hospital visitors parking lot, Wade shut off the motor and headed for the entrance.

Hearing loud voices from one of the examining rooms, Wade paused by the open door and listened to the patient yell.

"I tell you it was a spook that caused me to do it. I was cutting the haunches off an elk and I heard the gawd-awfulest noise you ever heard. It was an Indian war cry, if I ever heard one. He was ticked off at me for killing his game. It scared me so bad I almost cut off my hand. I ain't never going back there again, believe you me!" The scruffy individual was still pale; whether it was from loss of blood or fear, he didn't know. But the butchering incidents seemed to have been solved. The punishment seemed to be more than enough for the crime and, according to his laments, was unlikely to happen again. He listened a few seconds more until the doctor asked the man why he hadn't come in sooner. "Wasn't going to come in at all. Couldn't get it to stop bleeding," was the muttered answer.

That's both problems solved, Wade thought with satisfaction as he continued down the hall to the captain's room. "Jess was right. Kunes didn't butcher the yearlings." Picturing the man's reaction to the Indian war cry gave Wade's sense of humor a workout. He was still grinning as he pushed the captain's hospital door open.

Staring at the empty bed in consternation, Wade grabbed the orderly that came in to finish cleaning the room and barked, "Where is Captain Jessup?"

"He's gone," the man replied calmly. Wade let him go like he had hold of a hot stove lid "Oh Lord!" Wade groaned. "I thought sure he would be all right. He was looking good a few days ago, what happened?"

Noting Wade's shocked look and his sorrow, the man quickly said, "I don't mean that he died, I mean he checked out of the hospital this morning. Sorry, I gave you a scare. Didn't mean to do that, man."

Relief flooded through Wade as he gave a vast sigh of relief. He was very fond of his former captain and thought of him as a second father, more or less. The thought of never seeing him again would have left a huge hole in his life. He could have strangled the orderly for scaring him like that, but he knew he hadn't done it on purpose, so he let it go.

"Know where he went?" Wade asked as he headed for the door.

"Nope, might ask at the desk though. He would have to leave an address to send the bills to."

"Thanks," Wade responded on the way out.

The trip back to the station took longer than he intended. Wade stopped to help an elderly lady with a flat tire. Her spare was also down, and he had to have it fixed before he could put it on her car. He felt well paid when she hugged him with tears in her eyes and thanked him several times. She even had him bend down so she could plant a kiss on his cheek. Helping her into her car with a flourish and a wide grin, he waved the slightly stunned lady on her way.

"Wow," she muttered. "Seventy-eight and not dead yet!" She grinned happily as she headed home to tell Frank of her adventure with the ranger. 'Course she would leave a little bit out of the telling, but it wouldn't hurt the story any. "I'll save the memory of what that smile did to me, just for me!" She grinned contentedly. "Hot dog, that brings back memories!"

Pulling up in front of the station, Wade shut the motor off and sat trying to decide about what to do about Karnes. "He may never come back to this neck of the woods. Be a shame to keep Jess separated from his family any longer. Guess I better tell him to bring them home. There's no reasonable reason not to—the man's got me talking to myself like someone's grandma!" he muttered savagely.

Climbing out of the jeep, Wade entered the station and looked around. No one in sight. Heading for his office, he pushed open the door and headed for the fax to check for incoming, hoping for something on Karnes—nothing. Heading for the coffee machine automatically, he stopped and looked at the clean coffeemaker that was clearly empty. Nothing there either. Turning back to his office, he sat at his desk and looked around for mail—nothing.

"Corporal!" he yelled in frustration. The sound of something breaking in the bathroom gave him pause. At least the station hadn't been abandoned. Waiting for the occupant to emerge, he watched the bathroom door until it opened. Jess came out looking surprised and unsettled.

"Captain, you're hard on coffee cups. Keep that up and we'll have to buy more. Everything all right?"

"What are you doing with a coffee cup in the bathroom?"

"Not mine, I found it in there when I went in a while ago. I was getting ready to come out 'cause I thought I heard someone come in the front door and decided to take it to the kitchen. About the time I picked it up, you cut loose."

"Where's Corporal Kenyon?"

"She was a little under the weather, so I'm holding down the fort. Said it was a temporary thing."

"Oh." Wade said, his face coloring a bit. He turned away from Jess to hide it and headed back to his office. Pausing at the door, he said, "Jess, I don't think Karnes is anywhere near this area. I don't know where he is, but I think it's time you brought your family home. I think he wants me and will probably not go after anyone else. You can take precautions, but I believe it's safe enough for them. You can call them tonight and take the jeep for transport in the morning."

"Thanks, Captain, it's been pretty lonely at home. It will be great to have them home again!" The wide grin on Jess's happy face said it all. "You have an assignment for me for this afternoon?"

"No, you can have the rest of the day off. Go home and make your call."

'You bet, Captain. See you later," he hollered from the other side of the closing door."

"He can move when he wants to," Wade said grinning, as he noted that Jess hadn't put his parka on, just grabbed it and ran out the door with it in one hand and his hat in the other.

He sat in his chair and reached for a pad to make several notes to ask Lorraine in the morning when the phone rang. "Hello…? Captain Jessup…? How are you? I didn't know you were being released today. I just tried to visit you."

"I wasn't released Wade, I signed myself out of that place. It was running me buggy. Besides, I feel perfectly okay.

Doctor told me he was going to keep me for another week, I said, 'Oh no, you ain't!' How are things at the station?" he asked rather cautiously, Wade thought. Wondering what it was all about, Wade responded, "Everything's fine, Captain. You in a hotel room?"

"No, I'm staying with my sister June and her husband, Brad. They're April's parents. Soon as I'm able, I plan on going back to work. Is Kunes in prison for a while now, did they prove him guilty?" Jessup changed the subject, and Wade didn't push. The captain would let him know what he decided to do when he made up his mind.

"Yes, Captain, they did, they matched the bullets from the slaughtered elk with Kunes's rifle. He confessed to shooting Shade because he's the one that gave him away when he was hauling the elk carcasses from the park under the load of trees. He trashed my cabin because I arrested him for it. He stole your television because you got him fired from his job as groundskeeper at the university. He planned on doing a lot more, but he heard you coming and took off. He's in for quite a while, and hopefully, he'll learn something this time. If not, I guess we'll go around again when he gets out."

"Soon as I'm able, I plan on coming to the station for a visit. I am certainly grateful that the elk killer is behind bars. I have never been so angry about anything before. Well…glad everything's all right with you all. See you later, Wade."

The click in his ear stirred Wade from wondering about the obvious relief in Jessup's voice. Hanging up the phone, he looked around. Nothing to do. Looking at his watch, he decided to call it a day. Closing the station, he headed back to his cabin.

Stunned, Wade kept looking at the answering machine. Sometime today, he had received a call from Janine, the oldest of his sisters, and she wanted to know if he was coming back to the farm for Christmas. Today being December 20, it was in five days.

"Lord, where has the time gone?" he muttered in surprise. It seemed only last week that Jess had brought his family home, but it had been six weeks tomorrow if he counted right.

There was something like two feet of snow on the ground, and according to the forecast, more on the way and due to hit on the twenty-third. He wasn't about to get that far from home when a storm was brewing. The farm was a good three-hundred-plus miles from where he lived, and no one in their right mind traveled in a snow storm in Montana. Maybe he could pay a visit when the weather cleared.

Jess had requested a week off between Christmas and New Year's Day to take Sue and Patty to Willow Way to visit Peggy. Jerry was already gone having a family emergency, and he could not close the station to go visiting.

A case in point was the small plane that went down in the park just six weeks ago. He had found the wreck within hours, with Shade's help, in time to save the pilot's life. A broken leg, concussion, several broken ribs, and a bad case of hypothermia were what he found. It would have been a different story had he been found much later.

He knew that Corporal Kenyon could hold the fort for the two days that he would be gone. She was a very capable lady. With that in mind, he had gone with Jess to bring his family home. He smiled at the memory of the small avalanche that erupted from Peg's house when they pulled up in front and honked the horn. Shade was in top form again and was just as happy to see Jess and Wade as the rest of them were. Patty was still limping slightly but was cast-free and hugged them both numerous times. Shade finally gave up trying to get close to them and simply sat and panted happily. When things calmed down a bit later, he nudged Wade's hand and welcomed him with a wet kiss that he didn't have time to duck when he bent down to hug him.

Spending the night, they all piled into the jeep the next morning amid noisy good-byes and waves and happily headed home.

The trip back was noisy also, with four people and Shade packed in the jeep. Damp dog and the peppermint that Patty sucked on made him a bit claustrophobic for most of the trip home. In spite of that, it was fun, and Wade enjoyed the happiness that being together again made his friends. But he was very grateful when the trip ended.

Pulling up at the ranger station, Wade climbed out and let Jess have the jeep to drive to his cabin and unload luggage, people, and an ecstatic dog.

Checking into the station before heading for his cabin, he'd found Corporal Kenyon anxious to talk with him. She'd had a phone call from the state police about a small plane that went down in this area. The phone rang again as they were talking, and without a word, she handed it to Wade. Listening for a few seconds, he asked questions and soon hung up and barked, "Call Jess and anyone else in this area. I want them suited up, equipped for emergency search and rescue, and here in thirty minutes. I'll be right back. When you get that done, call everyone in the area and ask them if they heard a plane that sounded odd or heard a loud noise since yesterday. If you have any information that has a bearing on the search, call me on the two-way."

Making a hasty exit, he went to his cabin and followed his own instructions. Soon snowmobiles with sleds crisscrossed in ever-widening circles, and Shade rode on Wade's sled, lying down to stay on. His urgent barking had Wade stopping and letting him off. Following the dog as he struggled through the snow-laden pines soon brought them to the small clearing and a plowed-up ridge of snow with the plane under it. Digging, with Shade's help, soon uncovered the cockpit and the unconscious pilot. He had hit the radio soon as he found the plane and soon had more help from the other searchers.

They started arriving by the time he had the cockpit cleared of snow. Stabilizing the pilot's neck with rolled blankets from another sled, they splinted his leg and moved him gently to Wade's sled. Securing him to it took but a few minutes after they eased him into a down sleeping bag for the trip to the ranger station. Jess offered Shade a ride back to the station as Wade moved out slowly with his full sled. Calling ahead, he instructed Corporal Kenyon to call out for an Evac chopper. The packed area in front of the station was large enough for the chopper to land and did shortly after they arrived. The pilot was soon on his way to the hospital.

Heading back to his cabin for a cleanup, Wade's mind drifted to the time his Gram had been missing due to her horse falling into a snow-covered ditch and spraining its shoulder too bad for her to continue riding. She had stayed with a neighbor overnight to assist with the delivery of her son and was on her way back home the next morning when her horse fell. She had walked about two miles toward home, leading the badly limping chestnut when Wade found her. Inquiring into her health got him a brusque, "'Bout time you showed up. My cheeks are 'bout froze...all four of em!"

Their Gram being missing, even for a short time, was a bit traumatic as the loss of their parents were still vivid in their minds.

To get their minds off it, Gram popped corn and made hot chocolate. The smallest, Dale Evan, grabbed a handful and, grinning, stated firmly, "Pop corn!" then stuffed it into his mouth. It started to snow soon afterward, and Dale Evan stood looking out the picture window for a while then, turning to his gram grinning, said "Pop rain!"

There was no snow or sleet, just popped rain, frozen rain and rain.

Wade smiled at the memories of what used to be. Ironically, Dale was now a weatherman for one of Montana's television channels.

Shade went around remarking his territory soon as they returned to the station the second time, checking to see if there had been any intruders. Wade had checked in with Corporal Kenyon soon as they loaded the injured pilot and watched them lift off heading for Columbia Falls Hospital.

Nothing unusual in the mail, and Captain Jessup had called while they were gone to give and get an update on things. It was hard to believe that had been nearly six weeks ago. Calling Loraine's cabin, Wade waited impatiently for her to pick up. "Hello?"

"Corporal, have we had any mailers of upcoming events in town concerning Christmas lately?"

"Yes, Captain, there is one of the dance on Christmas Eve at the VFW hall in Columbia Falls. Why do you ask?"

"I've lost track of time, I was unaware that Christmas was so close. I was wondering if you would do me the honor of going to the dance with me?"

"Captain…are you asking me for a date?"

"Yes, Corporal, I believe I am…will you go?" Wade waited for her response with bated breath.

"I believe I would like to go to the dance with you, Captain, what time should I be ready?"

Letting out the breath he hadn't even been aware that he was holding, Wade said, "Great, I'll pick you up at five thirty. Thanks, Corporal."

"No problem," she muttered, hanging up the phone. Diving for her closet, she looked for something suitable for the Christmas dance. It had been ages since she'd a date. Her eyes lit on the dress that she had bought especially for the date she was to go on to celebrate her engagement. It had remained unworn as it had held too many disappointing memories, but those memories didn't seem to matter much anymore. Something—or someone, she corrected herself—had quite usurped them. It was, also, the answer to her need right now and seemed made for the occasion.

"Bingo!" she exclaimed happily and started looking for shoes and the rest of her outfit.

Wade calmly replaced the receiver, restraining the urge to give vent to another war cry...

17

"I had a good time this evening, Lorraine, thanks again for coming," Wade murmured as he opened the jeep door and helped her to alight.

"So did I, Captain," she replied as she slipped from the passenger seat and found herself in snow up to her ankles. Her dance shoes were definitely not made for walking in the snow, even if most of it was packed, but she had alighted into one of the unpacked areas. She had forgotten the boots she wore to the dance and left them there.

Seeing her difficulty, Wade simply scooped her up and headed for her, door ignoring her surprised squeak. His taking the three steps and depositing her on her doorstep, apparently with very little effort, had Lorraine swearing at herself for her lack of coherent thought, her insides doing a slow meltdown. Strong as an oak, she was not a small woman—and good-natured to boot, even a good dancer. Drat the man! Didn't the blasted man have any bad points? Thanking Wade for his rescue and taking her to the Christmas party, she fished her key out of her purse and, hastily unlocking her door, bid him good night and shut it between them.

Leaning on the inside of the door to get her wits together, she reached an unwanted conclusion. She was—blast it!—very much in love with her captain. Oak-tree strength, tall, well built, knock-your-socks-off-at-twenty-paces smile, and a good nature to boot—the whole works that made up Wade A. McKenna. She loved every gorgeous inch of him. Drat the man! Pulling off her wet slippers, she threw them toward the closet and, peeling off her coat, headed for the shower.

"Wonder what the *A* stands for?" she wondered out loud a few minutes later as she stepped into the shower. "Adonis...? Maybe I'll ask him. Couldn't be any worse than mine," she decided as she relaxed under the warm spray.

Watching the door for several seconds after Lorraine had disappeared behind it, Wade mused, "Something lit a fire under her. Wonder what it was. For a first date, it wasn't bad at all, even if I didn't get a good-night kiss...Next time, my little corporal," he murmured gently and left her to it.

"Well, Captain, you're looking good. Doctors give you the go-ahead on working yet?" Wade asked as he shook his former captain's hand.

"Nope, haven't seen one since I left the hospital. How's things coming along here?"

"Fine, Captain. Like some coffee?"

"I could use some. Any rolls left?" he asked hopefully.

"'Fraid not," Wade returned with a grin. "Jess was here until about an hour ago, need I say more?"

"Nope," Jessup sighed regretfully as he poured his coffee. Passing the file cabinets on his way back to Wade's desk, he peeked discreetly on top of the tallest file cabinet, and his brows climbed toward his hairline when he spied the papers that he told Wade about several weeks ago. Wade must have forgotten to check them out. That meant that he still had some explaining to do. Soon as the timing was right, he hedged.

"Captain, I was wondering what your middle initial stood for, what is it, if I'm not being too nosy?" Lorraine asked as she filed the latest reports.

"Why do you want to know?" Wade countered.

"People have a tendency to not tell anyone their middle name if it's awful. Is yours?" she returned with a smile to take the sting out of the question. "Mine's awful. Yours couldn't possibly be worse than mine."

"Huh! Bet mine has them both beat," Jessup muttered.

"Not likely. Care to bet on it?" Lorraine said saucily. "Why don't we all put a dollar in the kitty, and the one with the worse middle name wins the pot?" Lorraine asked, looking at each one in turn. Getting a nod from each, she put a small bowl on the desk and said, "Ante up!"

"Wait a minute," Jessup said. "We should include Wilma. She's is still one of us. We should call her and ask of she wants to participate in the drawing, agreed?"

Getting a nod from the others, Lorraine reached for the phone.

"Aunt Wilma's in," Corporal Kenyon said as she hung up the phone. She suggested that we make it five dollars instead of one. Make it worth her while to come after the pot. Okay with you all?"

Getting nods from everyone again, she put her five in and waited for the rest to add theirs. "Okay, age before beauty. Captain Jessup, you go first. What does the *H* stand for in your name?" Lorraine said, grinning expectantly. Everyone looked at Jessup and waited.

'It's Horatio," Jessup muttered.

"Good one. You're next, Wade. What does the *A* stand for?" Lorraine was enjoying herself immensely.

"Avon," Wade muttered, his neck going a shade darker.

"Not bad. Jess, the *E* in yours?"

"Eugene," he said unhappily.

"What was Wilma's—the *M* in her name—stand for?" Jess asked.

"Maybeline," Lorraine said.

"Okay, that leaves you, Corporal. What does the *T* stand for?" Jess asked, and they all looked expectantly at her.

Coloring prettily, Lorraine bravely stated, "Tillitha."

Looking at each other, they all silently agreed that she won the pot, hands down. Picking it up, Wade solemnly handed it to her.

Taking it, she muttered her thanks and sat down at her desk and tried to look busy. Jess turned back and opened his mouth to ask the forbidden question. Lorraine glaring at him silenced him before he could ask it. Snapping his mouth closed, Jess, for once, decided that discretion was called for this time. After all, it was better safe than sorry. With a sheepish grin, he left with the rest.

She was very glad when they got back to their visit with Captain Jessup. At least she now knew what Wade's middle initial was; she could stop wondering about it. Everyone also knew what hers was, she added glumly.

"His mother must have been an Avon lady at one time," she mused. Her own Aunt Tillitha had been. "Wonder where Tillitha came from? Well, back to work, if anyone teases me about it, I'll slug 'em," she promised herself grumpily.

An hour later she found herself daydreaming about her high school reunion last year. It was her tenth year since graduation, and she was looking forward to it very much. Pulling into a parking space by the VFW hall, she did a double take. The lit sign over the door proudly displayed, SENIOR RAT S. Someone had removed one of the *e*'s from the sign, probably a freshman.

Grinning at the memory, she checked the coffee pot—empty. It was too late in the day to make another pot, so she washed the coffee maker and cups, stacking them in the small drain, and turned off the kitchenette light. Picking up her finished work, Lorraine pulled at the file cabinet drawer and grunted when it wouldn't budge. It did have a tendency to stick sometimes. Laying the paperwork on top, she gave it a good yank with both hands and had the satisfaction of winning the battle, so to speak. Grabbing the papers again, she shuffled them into a neat stack and filed them in front of the drawer for later attention. Bending down, she watched as she slowly closed the door and discovered the warp in the metal side that caught a rough spot on the side of the drawer. Opening it again, she took a hammer from the small tool box under the sink and tapping the warp, corrected it enough to prevent it catching again, least she hoped so. Closing the drawer and opening it again was easy now, and satisfied, she returned the hammer, turned out the light, and headed for the captain's office.

With a light knock, she opened the door and froze. Wade was leaning back in his chair and sound asleep, his hand on his thigh and still wrapped around the coffee cup that had failed to keep him alert with its contents. Watching him for a few seconds, Lorraine enjoyed seeing him totally relaxed. It was a first, she thought. Gently removing the empty cup from his hand, she set it on the desk and, with a last thoroughly enjoyable look, regretfully shook Wade's shoulder, *The dratted man was gorgeous even when asleep!*

"Captain, wake up…Captain?"

Wade slowly opened his eyes, wondering where the heck he was. Then it sunk into his head that he was in his office and his corporal was trying to wake him up. "I'm awake, Corporal, thanks."

"Captain, everyone else has gone home, and I'm finished for the day, is there anything else you want before I leave?" she asked.

"Yeah, one more thing," Wade muttered. Crooking his finger, he reached out when she leaned forward to hear and, sliding his hand under her braid, pulled her gently to him and had a totally satisfying kiss. Stunned, she forgot to object, then didn't want to. When she didn't, he deepened the kiss until she grabbed his shoulders to keep upright, her knees failing in that department.

"Wow! I mean, why did you do that?"

"I liked *wow* better, and I did that because I have been wanting to since I first laid eyes on you. No offense meant—on the contrary, my intentions are strictly honorable. But fair warning, I intend to do it again, do you mind?" he asked hopefully.

Getting her balance again, she backed toward the door and, to her credit, only weaved once. "I'll let you know," she said shakily. Still a bit dazed, she went home and poured herself a shot of bourbon. She didn't even like the stuff, something left behind by Wilma, but she needed something to start her brain functioning again. She wondered if Wade knew that his former secretary had had a nip now and then. She found her still a bit shaken, apparently, the next morning. While fixing her breakfast, she looked down and found herself buttering her fingers instead of the toast.

"He's dangerous to even think about," she muttered in disgust as she dropped the half-buttered toast on her plate and went to the sink to wash off the butter.

Wade watched her leave, and getting up, he held in the war whoop that would have had her running back in to see what was killing him. Grabbing his hat, he shrugged into his parka and locked up the station. Taking a deep breath of the cold, pine-scented air, he grinned. *She didn't bust my chops. There is hope*, he thought happily. He could have floated over the snow the way he was feeling. Kicking the snow off his boots, he opened the door and went inside, still happily thinking about the kiss.

"Where could Karnes be? He couldn't just disappear off the face of the earth, but it seems as though he did just that," Wade asked himself as he watched the snow falling from a cloud-darkened sky. It had been coming down steadily since early morning. It didn't look as though it was intending to stop any time soon either, he thought gloomily. The New Year's dance at the VFW hall was in two days, and he didn't know if he was going to be able to take Corporal Kenyon to it in this mess. The kiss they had shared last week still burned in his mind, and he wanted to do it again—a good excuse, when he brought her home and when the clock struck midnight, two good excuses he thought happily. Then looking at the falling snow, he amended, "If I can make it to town."

Captain Jessup was talking about taking over the station again, his doctor objected, but Jessup liked his job and promised to stick to paperwork—no "in the field" work. He did, however, promise to wait for the doctor's permission. Having to settle for that, his doctor decided to wait as long as possible to give him more recovery time. Heart attack wasn't something to ignore when they were inconvenient.

That reminded Wade of the papers Jessup told him to check out. Getting up from his desk, he went into the lobby checked the top of the tallest file cabinet—nothing there. Checking the other two cabinets netted him the same and, shrugging, he decided that they must have been thrown away when Lorraine cleaned up. He would ask her when he seen her this evening. He had asked her to the New Year's Eve dance and she was to give him her answer this evening after she had time to make some calls.

Several days later, Lorraine, having arrived and found the lobby empty, was having a serious conversation with herself. She really did need to get something settled once and for all. "One," she said aloud, ticking the reasons off on her fingers, "when we kiss it's like sticking my finger in a light socket, my knees melt. Two, when he does that, my brain only operates on three cylinders, I simply can't think. Three, every time I get within reach of him, I want to jump on him and kiss his brains out. Four, ordinary mortal men didn't kiss like he did. Five, his charm is lethal—internal damage possible. Six, he's better looking than any man had a right to be. So, what am I going to do about all that? Simple…" She added, "Let him chase me until I catch him." The matter settled as far as she was concerned, Lorraine pulled her chair up to her desk and settled into her work.

Ranger Wade

She didn't see Wilma back into Wade's office quietly close the door or the extremely satisfied smile on her face. She was thrilled that Lorraine had finally found a man that she liked and respected. Her beauty and willowy body had generated a lot of male attention from the wrong kind, and she had been in a habit of rejecting her suitors long enough that Wilma was afraid she would never find a husband. Apparently, that problem was solved, if what she just overheard meant what she thought it did.

Waiting for a few moments, she opened the captain's office door noisily and greeted Lorraine warmly. "Hello, sugar, it's good to see you. How do you like working here? The boys aren't giving you a hard time, are they?" she asked innocently as she gave her a hug.

Lorraine jumped and turned to see her Aunt Wilma looking quite well and with a strange look on her face.

"Aunt Wilma, I didn't know you were here. When did you arrive? Are you coming back to work?"

"Not yet, dear. If I do, it will be in the spring some time. My doctor isn't ready to let me do that yet. You're looking well, being a ranger suits you. It really does. Where is the captain? I arrived almost an hour ago and waited in his chair, but I believe I fell asleep. I didn't hear you come in."

Or anything else either, Lorraine hoped fervently. "I believe captain McKenna is in Columbia Falls visiting a friend in the hospital who had a skiing accident yesterday, and it almost killed him. He shouldn't have been doing that anyway. The man is nearly sixty years old, for Pete's sakes!

"That's not so old," Wilma protested. "I believe people should do what they feel like doing. One doesn't quit playing because one gets old. One gets old because one quits playing, don't you think?"

"I believe you are right, Aunt Wilma, I stand corrected," Lorraine agreed with a smile at the spunky lady's defense of her age group.

"How long can you stay? Will you come to my cabin for lunch? I have a casserole ready to put in the oven for dinner if you can stay overnight."

"I would love to, sugar, but I wanted to see the captain, and I've already been here longer than I planned on. I have an appointment with my doctor, and I promised to go the movies with my niece Kitty. Tell the captain that I'll come back when I have more time. It's so good to see you again, dear, take care."

Following her to the door, Lorraine was surprised to see her climb into a four-wheel drive pickup and wheel it expertly down the road.

Settling back in her chair, Lorraine picked up where she left off earlier. The dance had been, to quote a phrase, a blast! The heavy new snow layer had kept Wade from driving out to the dance, so he had made do, so to speak. Making a call to a friend, he picked Lorraine up on his snowmobile after telling her to dress warm and bring her party clothes along in a sack, and they met his friend where the main roads had been cleared of snow and went to the party with him. They reversed the procedure the next morning, having spent the night with said friend and his wife.

Wade had worn his ranger uniform as he didn't own a suit, and Lorraine had glared at hopeful females as they looked longingly at him. He has disappointed them all as he danced all his dances with Lorraine, to her vast satisfaction. She has imagined him dancing with other ladies and herself getting an occasional dance with him. It was, however, not to be. He was all hers for the duration. He had taken full advantage of the midnight kiss, melting her knees to the point that he had to hold her up for a while afterward. He didn't seem to mind that a bit, she thought wryly. Then to top it off, he had done the same thing again after delivering her to her door the next morning. It was a good thing that it was New Year's Day and no work. It took her the entire day to get her brain back to working on all cylinders.

I really do need to get some work done, she thought as she looked abstractedly at the papers on her desk. She wasn't seeing them though. Wade's smiling face imposed itself between her and her work. "I need coffee," she decided. Maybe a jolt of caffeine would help.

Jess came in while she was pouring herself a cup and she reached for another cup.

"Thanks, Lorraine," he murmured as he took the cup. "You seen Wade this morning?" he asked, taking a drink while checking the table for rolls.

"He's in town visiting a friend at the hospital. He said he would return around noon, give or take."

"Okay, I'll see if Sue needs any 'Honey, do' stuff done then. I'll be back later." He grinned as he sat his half-finished coffee on her desk and left.

Smiling absentmindedly at his retreating back, Lorraine's mind was once more full of the man that had changed her mind about men in general.

Shoving back her chair, she took Jess's cup back to the kitchenette and went to the file cabinet, taking out the papers in front to finish up.

"Captain, I believe I've found the papers that you were looking for." Lorraine said as he walked in and shrugged out of his parka. Sailing his hat at the rack, he didn't wait for it to catch but headed for the coffee pot. She explained about the stuck drawer and laying her papers on top to use both hands to get it open. "I must have picked them up along with the others and filed them."

"Thanks, Corporal, I'll look at them in a minute. I have to make arrangements for a guest at my cabin. Can you have an extra bed delivered by tomorrow? My friend is from New Mexico and in no shape to travel that far to get home. He will be staying with me until he recovers enough to do so."

"I'll see what I can do, but, Captain, isn't your couch a pull-out queen sleeper? Oh, and Jess was looking for you earlier. He said he would try again later."

"He's coming now," Wade murmured, looking out the window. "Send him in when he gets here, and forget about the bed, the couch will do. I forgot about it being a sleeper. I've never used it." Gathering the papers on Lorraine's desk, he retreated to his office and shut the door.

A few minutes later, Jess knocked on Wade's door and, opening it, stopped. His captain was reading papers that had him dumbfounded from the look on his face. Slapping them down on the desk, Wade looked at Jess without really seeing him and growled, "All that worrying and shipping your family off for nothing. The man had been dead…dead! All this time. What in thunder was Captain Jessup thinking to keep this from me? Jess…sorry, man. Here, read this." Handing the papers to Jess, he waited until he read them and laid them on his desk. Looking at Wade, he cleared his throat and said, "Looks as if your problem is solved—that one anyway. You mean Captain Jessup knew about this and didn't tell us?"

When Wade nodded, Jess muttered, "He better have a darn good reason. I lived in an empty house for six weeks because of him."

"I am going to town to pick up my friend from the hospital day after tomorrow, I plan on leaving early so I can stop and have a little talk with Captain Jessup. I'll find out what happened to cause him to with hold the information from us, and it had better be good," he muttered as he read the papers again.

> Captain Jessup
>
> I am writing you to inform you that you can disregard the warning about Karnes that I sent you earlier. The accident, mentioned in the last letter that happened to one of the inmates, happened when a large piece of equipment fell into a sinkhole, trapping the driver for several hours. He was freed and will be fine, but it was noted that Karnes had disappeared at the same time. We assumed that he had used the accident to escape. However, three days later while removing the equipment from the sinkhole, Karnes was found at the bottom of the sinkhole. He must have been standing too close, and when it went, it took him with it. Included is a copy of his death certificate.
>
> I hope this relieves your mind about Karnes.
>
> Sincerely,
Warden James T. Keller
Montana State Prison
Deer Lodge Valley

Looking up, Wade noted that Jess had left. Putting the papers down, he ran his hand through his hair and gave a deep sigh that came from somewhere in the vicinity of his boots. Better that he wouldn't see the captain for a day or two; give him time to cool off. "No wonder he was wary of me after he told me about the papers on the file cabinet," Wade growled, glaring at the papers. Then, checking his watch, he headed for his cabin and a late lunch.

Ranger Wade

The VFW hall was beautifully decorated for the Easter party near the end of March. A play was enacted of the Crucifixion and resurrection of Jesus by the local high school seniors, and Wade thought that they did a credible job. A small boy even ran up on the stage and kicked the soldier that was whipping Jesus in the shin and had to be removed. The audience roared; even the whipped Jesus grinned at his pint-sized champion. His mother grabbed him before he could inflict more damage to the unfortunate soldier's shin.

Wade and Lorraine were still smiling when the play ended, and they joined the line for the buffet. Wade had relaxed and was a better date now that Karnes wasn't on his mind. He had forgiven his captain for not informing him when he got the letter, but Captain Jessup explained that he wanted the elk killer caught in the worse way and he figured that Wade would work all the harder if he figured it was Karnes that he was after. Unfortunately, he was laid low with his heart problem before the elk killer was caught, and he did—he reminded Wade—try to inform him about Karnes as soon as he heard about the elk killer's capture. It wasn't his fault that Wade forgot to check out the papers on the file cabinet. He did admit that he figured letting him know in this manner would give Wade time to cool off a bit before he faced him with it. Captain Jessup did show up at the Easter gathering.

Wilma was also present, accompanied by Wade's friend, Delbert Lansing, who had had the skiing accident. Wilma was introduced to him on one of her visits to the ranger station, and they had hit it off instantly from the start. She didn't care for the name Delbert and called him Del. He hadn't returned home as planned soon as he was able. Indeed he had rented a cabin and was seeing Wilma regularly and, if things went as he planned, would soon ask Wilma to be his wife. He had told her that he worked on a ranch but neglected to tell her that he owned said ranch and was in fact a multimillionaire. He wanted to be sure that she wanted him for himself, not his money. He decided to marry her when she became worried that he was broke and offered to lend him some money till he was back to work.

Wade overheard her low-voiced offer of assistance and nearly choked on his coffee. Delbert looked at him and shook his head slightly, letting him know that he didn't want her to know yet. Nodding slightly, Wade got his breathing under control and assured Wilma that he was okay. He had some serious courting to do himself. He planned to ask Lorraine to marry him when he took her home this evening. He had the ring in his pocket, having asked Wilma for her ring size.

I believe Aunt Wilma is about to be proposed to, if I read her friend's body language correctly. That means that she won't be coming back to the ranger station this spring, Lorraine thought. *I'll have to ask Wade to find another secretary. I certainly have no intentions of doing that for much longer. I need to return to the field. I'm no more an inside ranger than Wade is.*

Pulling up in front of her cabin that evening when he took her home, Wade asked if he could come in for a cup of coffee. Still in a party mood, Lorraine readily agreed, and soon as they were inside, she hung her jacket and headed for the kitchen.

"Lorraine," he called, stopping her in her tracks. His voice sounded strange, like he was having trouble getting her name out. Stopping in front of her, Wade looked at her, stumped as to how one went about proposing.

Shifting from one foot to the other, Wade tried desperately to find the words he wanted to say. Fascinated, Lorraine watched him squirm. If this meant what she thought it might, she wanted it to come from him.

"Yes, Wade?" she prompted gently.

Lord, I must have left my brains in my other hat! he thought desperately. *I'd been so busy running from females that when I did the chasing and caught one, I don't know what to do with her.*

Looking up, he silently pleaded, *Please?* The Lord must have helped him, for he suddenly thawed out and, placing his hands on her shoulders, looked into her beautiful eyes and handed his heart to her. "I love you Lorraine, I'm not much, but what I am is all yours, will you marry me?"

Letting him squirm for all of ten seconds while she silently disagreed with his estimate of his own worth, Corporal

Lorraine T. Kenyon said with a straight face, ignoring her thundering heart, "I'll think about it."

Somehow, Wade never thought how he would respond if she turned him down, and this wasn't a firm no…but it wasn't the yes he was hoping for either. Then noting the twinkle in her eyes, he, also with a straight face, slowly began to advance toward her.

Lorraine's eyes widened. And as she turned to run, he caught her around the waist; and before she knew it, he had her trapped against his hard, massive chest and was kissing the life out of her. Gasping for breath, she quickly exclaimed, "I surrender, I'll marry you…don't quit!" He grinned and started to release her, having accomplished his aim.

Grabbing her again, Wade planted his best kiss yet on her willing lips, and when he let her go, had to catch her. Her knees had melted for sure this time. "I'll give you a week to stop that," she murmured huskily.

Sitting her in a chair, he kissed her again and was going back for a third when she protested. "Wade, I'll never walk again if you keep that up!" Grabbing his arm, she stood and put her arms around his neck and murmured, "We'll have plenty of time to see how fast you can melt my knees in the future. For now, you better leave before people start talking about us. I have my reputation to think of—and yours also," she added.

"No one around to see us," he murmured planting another long, internal-damage-type kiss on her all-too-willing lips.

"We still should stop…," she demurred, clinging to his jacket with both hands.

"My week isn't up yet," he protested.

"While we still can," she added.

"What about the rest of my week?" he asked, quirking an eyebrow.

"To be continued," she returned with a wicked grin.

Wade reluctantly let her go after a last lingering kiss and, pulling on his jacket, opened the door. And with a last look, he left, shutting the door gently. Lorraine stood for a bit, soaking in the happenings of the day. Then with a grin, she simply let go.

Wade paused on the porch, and a smile split his face from ear to ear. He had done it! She said yes, and he was the happiest man alive, bar none. Still grinning, he slapped on his hat and started to step off the porch and took all three steps at the same time when the feminine version of a war whoop split the air.